dear reader,
I hope you like this book!
happy reading!
James

James
Brown

# THE DREAM THIEF

Steven Glass was asleep. Lost to the waking world, he drifted weightless through the simmering cauldron of his dreams. Images appeared in his mind's eye, unfurling like flags before the burgeoning wind.

He saw a rough well of stone in a small garden, blinding light pouring forth from the brim. A pale gleam of silver in the lurking shadows of an abandoned hall. A mask-like face, white and twisted, chortled maliciously above a bulging black sack. Three figures waited on high thrones, shrouded in golden mist, and a doorway opened onto a beckoning path.

Steven drifted on the tide, tugged this way and that, turning over and over like a swimmer basking in the current. In his bed, his eyes flicked to and fro beneath his closed lids as he murmured softly to himself. In the land of dreams, the endless ribbon of mysteries enshrouded him.

Somewhere a clock was ticking. He glimpsed slender black hands separating seconds from minutes, carving minutes from hours; an inexorable succession of moments melting into the eternal present.

It was here! The clock was before him, a high sweep of burnished metal, glowing like a beacon in the darkness. Stretching out a hand, he longed to brush his fingertips against it, to touch its magnificent design. He felt movement like the brush of a bird's wing about him and knew that Time itself was here; it was all around, sliding through him like oil.

It was almost midnight.

Steven turned over in his bed.

Quiet was the house around him. A cup brimming with water, it held in stillness.

The clock struck twelve.

Clear were the chimes, high up in the eaves, sounding out like ripples of molten silver. Gliding over the black wave of the night, they rang out; and out; and out.

In Steven's dream the moment held tight between the old day and the new. Held – and locked.

The luminous ribbon passing through his mind stretched as though hooked, strained fiercely like a lion on a leash– and tore.

*Wake up!*

The words rang in his ears.

*Wake up!* Again the words resounded in his mind. His dream receded away, shredding like tissue paper. Desperately, he grasped after it, but his fingers closed on empty air.

*Wake up!*

The pain of it, like a wound burning in his side.

He woke.

With a lurching gasp he sat upright, green eyes wide and staring. His hair was matted against his forehead. He was drenched in sweat, his T-shirt clinging to him like a moist hand.

For a moment or two he gazed around, at a loss as to where he was. The eddying fragments of the dream were still spinning away and he was like a spar of driftwood caught in the turbulence.

Then, slowly, he began to make out the familiar contours of his bedroom; his wardrobe, his desk, the small pool table with the cues askew over the baize. The dim light of a streetlamp filtered through the heavy curtains.

It was a dream. That was all. Just a dream.

His breath came loud in the stillness; uncertainty prickled the base of his neck.

Something seemed out of place, and it took him a moment to realise what it was.

The house itself was silent.

It wasn't just quiet, as you'd expect a house to be at midnight. No, it was utterly silent, as totally without noise as if someone had rendered him instantly deaf.

Steven always heard vague noises when he was in bed; creaking from the walls and ceiling, the distant thump of pipes carrying water to and fro. If not that, then the faint murmur of traffic from the nearby road, or the wind and rain washing over the house like a descending curtain.

Now there was only his heartbeat, fast inside his chest. The faint itch on his neck came again, like a hard finger prodding. Something was out of joint.

He got out of bed.

He looked fairly unremarkable, Steven, slightly taller than most, with a pleasant face and a look of slight distance about him, as though he was always thinking about something else. He was a dreamer by nature, often caught gazing out of the window during lessons, entranced by the movement of the clouds or the wind stirring the leaves on the trees. Walking home, he could be arrested by the sight of a delicate frond of ice on a windowpane, the intricate architecture of a spider's-web that had somehow appeared overnight. The concrete, the everyday, the tangible passed him by like froth thrown up by the tide.

The only unusual thing about him was his sharp green eyes that sometimes clouded over when he was deep in thought.

They were clouded over now.

The carpet felt soft under his feet as he crossed to the window and drew back the curtains. He peered out of the window at the night sky.

It was black, and the clouds hung like wisps of crepe. The moon was as round and flat as a plate. It suddenly came to him that he could reach out and push the scene over with one finger: it looked about as real as a picture on a greeting-card.

Then a sudden thought struck him.

*Am I sleepwalking again?*

As a child he often drifted about the house in the middle of the night, eyes half-open, murmuring softly until his mother or father guided him back to bed. Once or twice he had even ventured outside, and had been found examining the hedgerows and pavements as though he were an anthropologist intent on unearthing the remains of some ancient civilization.

He couldn't be sure. He didn't *feel* like he was sleepwalking, but how would you know if you were?

He stood for a minute, uncertain, then pinched himself.

*Ow!*

'Well...' he said to the silence.

Creeping softly out of his room, he went out into the hall.

A grandfather clock was there. It was Steven's favourite thing in the house. Ever since he was a boy it had stood like a silent guardian at the summit of the stairs, keeping watch over him. There had once been a time when he had gazed up at the smooth oak panels and gleaming clock-face and been reassured by the steady, even ticking. Even now he was older he still found comfort in the inevitable movement of the clock-hands and the steady drumbeat of Time.

He squinted against the dim light. He might have been under the surface of the ocean, peeping up at the moon.

The clock's hands were stopped at midnight.

Just like his dream.

*This is very strange*, he thought. *Very strange indeed.*

*Was it wound properly?* Better be sure.

The clock needed seven turns to the right with its small silver key to keep it wound. Quietly, he undid the front of the cabinet.

The key was missing.

A thrill of wonder and fear, as sheer and dense as lightning, shot through him. It left the taste of old pennies in his mouth.

Then that feeling of wrongness tugged at him again.

*Better wake Mum and Dad!*

He crept over to the door of his parents' bedroom and raised his hand to knock.

His arm locked in mid-air.

Steven couldn't move it. Not one inch. There was no pain, no sense of being held. Just the sense that an invisible barrier had sprung up between his hand and the door.

He let his hand drop, waited a moment. Then tried again.

It was the same. Try as he might, Steven could not make his hand reach the wooden door of his parents' bedroom.

*Alright then*, he thought.

Moving swiftly, not bothering to be quiet now, he went back to his room and changed, pulling on an old sweater and a pair of jeans. Stuffing his feet into his trainers, he peered into the mirror in his wardrobe, doing his best to tug his unruly brown hair into submission.

A coat? No, he didn't think so. It was warm enough.

Actually, it wasn't really warm at all. It just wasn't cold either.

It was – nothing.

Taking nothing else with him, he went down the stairs, closing up the grandfather clock as he went.

He took hold of the front door handle.

Steven's father locked it every night before he went to bed. The keys could be anywhere. It was as much to stop Steven sleepwalking outside as anything else; and yet he knew, as he put his hand out, that it would open for him.

He turned the handle and the door swung out without a sound.

Pallid moonlight lay over the street, an insubstantial sheet of glossy paper. The air was flat and dull. There were no stars.

Steven took a deep breath as he stepped over the threshold, and he closed the door behind him.

The road was deserted. Steven was alone.

The fullness of the night sky was spread out high above, and yet it was the same as his glimpse of it from upstairs; insubstantial, more for show than real, the faded circle of moon and hanging threads of cloud reminding him only of jaded Christmas decorations the day after Boxing Day, when the batteries had run out on his presents and everyone was tetchy after too many mince pies and too much turkey.

Everything felt so – empty, deserted like some abandoned mausoleum. Yet it still looked the same, the car, lovingly polished every Sunday by his Dad, his Mum's prize rosebushes blooming at the edge of their small garden.

*Is anyone else awake?*

It didn't seem like it. He could be the only one.

*Everyone else is asleep?*

He could go to another house and knock on the door. He didn't know his neighbours very well, however, and midnight was certainly an odd time to be calling. Although this wasn't exactly a normal situation to find himself in...

The house next door squatted impassively, curtained windows seeming to glare outwards at the night.

*Maybe not, then.*

*What now?*

Some small part of his mind, still unwilling to believe he was not having a particularly vivid dream, said, *you need to wake up.*

It could be true.

There were ways to test that. Licking his finger he held it up in the air, expecting to feel a breeze on it. He stood there for a moment, waiting.

Nothing.

Even at night, there should have been *something*.

He crouched down by the rosebushes. The thin stems rose up from the rich earth, red petals swelling outwards, curved thorns ready for the unwary.

Steven pressed his finger against one.

It didn't hurt. It felt somehow limp, like it was made of rubber. It might have been a decoration in a funhouse for all he felt.

He pressed harder.

Still nothing. The thorn didn't scratch him.

'Hmmm,' he murmured to himself, tugging his bottom lip between thumb and forefinger.

Then – *sorry, Mum* – he tried pulling one out. Unmindful of the thorns, he wrapped two hands around the stem, gripped tight, and yanked upwards.

He couldn't do it. It was like pulling on a root embedded a hundred miles into the earth. It simply refused to budge.

'Come – on!' Steven gritted his teeth, straining, feeling an answering tug in his back.

No good. He growled in frustration and thrust the flower away from him, where it bobbed back and forth like a spring for a few moments before coming gently to rest in exactly the same position as before.

His palms were throbbing and he wiped them on his jeans.

'Now what?' he muttered.

'I could have told you that wouldn't work,' came a voice.

Steven jumped in shock. He hopped half a foot in the air and gasped in a huge breath at the same time, which made him croak like a frog as he whirled around.

*Who said that?*

No-one was there. The street was still deserted.

'Great, I'm hearing things now,' he said.

'You're not going mad,' came the voice again. It was slow and rich, with an odd sort of drawl at the end, as if the owner had seen it all before. It was the voice of someone faintly bored, trying to explain something to someone who just wasn't getting it.

Some feet away, perched on top of a delicate-looking birdbath, sat a large cat with piercing yellow eyes. It was looking at him.

It had fur as black as velvet, with delicate splashes of white across its paws and the tip of its tail. Another patch spread over its cheeks and forehead, like a thrown snowball.

'You...you didn't...' Steven knew that his mouth was hanging open foolishly, but he couldn't seem to do anything about it.

'I did indeed,' the cat said, its lips parting smoothly and a bright pink tongue peeping out. 'And close your mouth, please. You look like an idiot.'

Deftly, it sprang down from the birdbath and came towards him.

Steven was still gaping. 'You...you're talking!'

The cat sighed. 'If I explain quickly, it'll be a lot easier.

'Number one, yes, I'm a cat, and yes, I can talk. Number two, you're Steven, and you need to come with me.

'And number three, we don't have a lot of time, so please hurry up.'

Steven felt a sudden rush of dizziness, a whirling in his head that left his legs quivering like jelly, and suddenly, without realising how, he found himself sitting down.

The upside of this was that he felt better. The downside was that he was that much closer to the cat's disconcerting stare.

'It's like this,' it purred. 'You're not dreaming. You are, in fact, the only one awake at this point in time. In fact, unless you come with me, you're likely to be the only one awake for a very *long* time.'

It sat down daintily by his side. 'I realise this may be difficult for you.'

'Yes,' Steven said weakly, 'you could say that.'

'Well, if it's any consolation, it's no joke for me either,' the cat said. 'Do I look like I want to be wandering around in the middle of the night, chasing up strange children?'

Steven didn't have an answer for that. Maybe after he'd met a few more talking animals, he'd have a better idea of what they were supposed to be doing roaming the streets at all hours.

He rubbed a hand along the back of his neck. At length, he said, 'What's going on?'

The cat blew out a long breath. 'It's tricky to say, exactly. Let's just say something – or some *things* – are going missing, and you're in a position to – grant us some aid, so to speak. Does that help?'

'Well, er, no,' Steven said. 'Not exactly. Sorry.'

'Never mind,' the cat said. 'Let's be going.'

'Going?' Steven asked. 'Going? Where are we going? I don't see your car anywhere!'

He laughed suddenly, shrilly, and the cat gave him a funny look.

'I mean, I've got nothing against cats,' Steven went on in a high-pitched voice, 'although I'm more of a dog person really, I think they make better pets although I've never actually had one, I always used to say to my Mum and Dad we should...'

His voice petered out under the electric gaze of those yellow eyes.

'Steven,' the cat said softly, 'it really is better if you just do what I say for the time being. And I promise you will understand in a little while. Okay?'

Steven took a deep breath, swallowed nervously, and nodded.

'Right then,' the cat said, and it tapped one paw three times on the ground.

All at once the space between them began to shimmer and sway. It was like a heat haze had suddenly appeared out of thin air, and as Steven blinked and tried to clear his vision he felt the ground beneath his feet begin to quake.

'What's happening?' he cried. 'What's going on?'

The cat grinned at him. Even in the moon's thin light Steven could see it had small, pointed teeth.

There came a sharp crack as though a beam of wood had snapped and before his astonished eyes a rip appeared in the air, a bright tear in the fabric of reality. Bright light poured through, dazzling him.

'Hang on!' the cat called. 'Don't be afraid!'

Steven didn't even have time to be scared. The tear spread wide, and as the ground leapt up under him he shot into the enveloping light.

'Where am I?' Steven whispered.

An enormous pair of wooden doors stood before him, seamed as ancient bark. They towered above his head, solid and forbidding.

The burst of white light had lasted only a moment. Already the feeling was passing away, fading from his memory like stepping off a rollercoaster: as soon as your feet touch the ground, the feeling of giddiness and excitement begins to fade...

The cat was by his ankles.

'We go in,' it whispered.

Deep within the wood of the doors strange designs had been carved, looping and swirling like the trails of fish dancing through deep water. They looked remote and alien, constellations from a distant galaxy. Steven tried to focus on them, to make them out clearly, but at the edges of his gaze they seemed to swirl, moving to an unknown tune he could not hear.

The cat pressed a paw against the doors.

In silence, they swung open.

'Follow me,' the cat said. It went inside.

A step behind, Steven followed.

Beyond, a vast space opened. Pale marble was beneath his feet, and at the edges of the echoing darkness Steven sensed huge pillars of stone rising overhead.

A fine golden mist rose up to meet him. It came billowing forward, a ghostly luminescence that seemed to eddy in an invisible wind, and Steven took a step backward. Was it dangerous?

'Don't be afraid,' the cat whispered. 'It's safe.'

With an effort, Steven remained still and let the mist touch him. Golden threads brushed over his face, as gentle as a dragonfly, and he smelled a strange, dry odour, like old lemons.

There came a soft, easy sigh from around him and the mist rolled back across the floor.

'I have brought him,' the cat said to the emptiness.

*Who is it speaking to?* Steven wondered.

In the next moment light began to swell. It was as if the entire room was a lamp, a lamp gradually brightening, and a warm nimbus of illumination shrank the shadows back.

Three figures appeared, seated atop high thrones of gleaming metal. They gazed down at Steven.

In the centre was a woman. Enthroned in silver, her dark robe cascaded down to the stone floor. Her hair, white as coral, fell to her shoulders in a gleaming tapestry. Her face, young and unlined, was open and welcoming; and yet her eyes were deep, as old and unfathomable as the ocean.

To her right was a burly man on a throne of gold. His hair was russet, curling beneath his ears, and a bristling beard garlanded his powerful jaw. His robe was red and yellow and green and blue, and the colours spilled over each another like an artist's running palette. He was smiling faintly, and his grey eyes were full of a dancing good humour.

The third figure was on a throne of ebony. It wore a black robe with the cowl pulled down so low, Steven couldn't tell if it was a man or a woman. Looking at it made him shiver. There was something of a spider's thinness in the shrouded limbs, and the shadows still clung to it even in the light, as though it were reluctant to relinquish them.

The three figures seemed somehow familiar, as though he had seen them before somewhere, read about them in a tome of knowledge, glimpsed them fleetingly in some long-forgotten dream. There was something of power about their limbs and eyes, their burnished thrones; a vast force that beat out like heat from a roaring fire.

'Welcome, Steven,' the woman said. Her voice was like the pealing of a silver bell. She spoke softly but Steven heard her as clearly as if she had been by his side.

Upon hearing her words a wave of warmth went through him, as though he had slipped into a deliciously heated bath. He straightened up and squared his shoulders, smiling back. 'Hello.'

'Welcome, Sleepwalker,' the man said, inclining his head. Again, although he spoke quietly, his rich tones echoed in Steven's ears like the creaking of mighty branches in the warm summer wind.

The figure in black made no sound.

'Where am I?' Steven asked. To his own ears, he sounded thin and tremulous.

'Somewhere east of the moon, east of the sun,' the woman replied.

The cat, meowing softly, sprang up onto her lap. Even though she sat far above the floor, it made the jump without apparent effort.

The woman began to stroke its back. 'I see you have met my friend here.'

'Yes,' Steven said. 'Or he met me, you could say.'

'We regret we had to bring you here so suddenly,' she went on. 'There was no time to prepare you.    You see, we need your help.'

'Me?' Steven coughed. 'What do you expect me to do? How can I possibly help?' He was only a boy! Surely there was some mistake?

'You must help us,' the russet-haired man implored. 'This is something only you can do, Sleepwalker.'

*Sleepwalker? How does he know I used to sleepwalk?*

'There is a thief abroad!' the woman exclaimed sternly. 'He prowls the land, sneaking here and there, snatching away what is not his. He must be stopped.'

'What's – what's he stolen?' Steven said. What on earth would someone be stealing here? Somehow he doubted there were mobile phones around, or enormous widescreen TVs.

Then suddenly, he knew.

His dream. The clock frozen at midnight, the agonising tear as his dream was ripped away.

'It's dreams,' Steven said softly. 'It's dreams, isn't it?'

The figure in black laughed abruptly. Steven flinched at the sound. It was sharp and cold, and grated in his ears like a sharp talon being scraped against a windowpane.

'Yes, it is dreams,' the woman went on. 'He steals them away from their rightful dreamers. To do this, he has stopped the great Clock, the Clock of Hours that marks all Time. This is – not allowed. There are certain powers here, Steven, immutable forces that keep everything balanced. If they are broken…'

'You live twice each day, Steven,' the man said, 'once during the daylight hours, in waking, in your world. At night, you live again here, in the Dreamland. You need your dreams as much as you need your waking hours…and if your dreams are taken, misfortune and ill chance can only follow, which will not be without consequence in your world also.'

'Yes,' Steven said slowly. 'I understand that. I think – I think he came to me too. Stole a dream, I mean.'

The woman and man glanced at one another, brows furrowed, and the figure in black laughed again.

'But – what can I do?' Steven wanted to know. 'I don't even know where to start!'

With a silky spring, the black-and-white cat was on the floor before him once more.

'My companion here will go with you,' the woman said. 'His name is Orion. He will guide you in your task, and we will give you what aid we can, where we can.'

The burly man leaned forward, his eyes piercing. 'You only have a short time, Sleepwalker. The longer the great Clock remains frozen, the more dreams he will steal.

'Now you must go. It will not be easy – but take heart!'

Suddenly, the room began to darken. He started forward, stretching out a hand. 'Wait! Wait - who are you?'

'You will learn our names, in time,' the woman said. Her outline was growing soft and hazy and her words reached him as if over a great distance. 'In time…'

Before him the room grew smaller, the three figures shrinking.

'Wait!' Steven called a last time. 'Don't go!'

'Travel well, Sleepwalker,' came the faint reply. 'Travel well…'

Then they were gone.

'*Aaaah!*' he cried.

Instantly Steven had to clap a hand over his eyes. Colours burst in front of him, whirling, blinding, a fractured mirage of light that was so intense and powerful he needed to push it away to stop himself going blind.

With his fingers pressed over his eyes, blissful darkness returned. After a moment's hesitation, he tried opening his fingers slightly, then clenched them shut again instantly. He couldn't *see!*

It was as if a mad painter had smashed a prism into a thousand pieces, ground the remains in a pestle, and slung the fragments into a pulsing, throbbing rainbow.

Colour blurred into colour; hue ground against shade; light spun away from dark. It was beautiful, awful, maddening.

It was too much.

'*Help! I can't see!*'

*Where was Orion? Where was he?*

Then he heard a meow by his ankles. 'Sorry! I always forget.'

The pressure of a paw against his calf. 'There! Try that.'

A cool, languid feeling rose up from where Orion had touched him. It was like a gentle press of water, spreading through his body, smoothing, soothing. At he felt it reach his head Steven gradually lowered his hands from his eyes.

He could see again. The overwhelming maelstrom of colour had vanished.

They were standing on the brow of a hill, overlooking a patchwork of green fields and meadows.   There were wild-looking forests descending into deep valleys; the glittering waters of lakes and the winding threads of paths. On the distant horizon blue-hazed mountains jutted up to the sky.

Yet it was still different.

Because everything was shifting.

As Steven watched in disbelief, the entire landscape moved. A meadow suddenly collapsed, folding into itself like a scrunched-up handkerchief, before turning inside out again into a murky swamp that gave off throaty belches of gas. The flowing waters of a stream abruptly leapt into the air and became a long stretch of cloud that drifted serenely away towards the hills.

Steven felt like he was standing on the edge of a deep drop. He struggled to keep his footing, but any moment now the edge would tilt away from him and he would plunge down and be lost. It was moving – he was falling – *falling* –

He brought his hands up to cover his eyes again – and realised that he could see straight through them.

At first glance they appeared completely normal; pink skin and slender fingers, a small scar at the base of his thumb where he had caught himself on a rusty nail in his Dad's shed. Then the skin dissolved away like smoke and he could see his veins and tendons running through his flesh, like some crazy road-map of pink, purple and blue.

Then that, too, was gone, and he could see his bones. The actual bones of his hands.

'Er - '

Crouched by his side, Orion looked up, saw the expression of his face, and hurriedly tapped his ankle again. 'Oops! Sorry – it doesn't often take two –

There was a twitch around Steven's eyes and something firm and dark descended, pressing over his face like he had put on a pair of thick sunglasses.

Blessedly, everything stopped moving. The fields stayed as fields. The lakes were still. Steven looked at his hands again. This time they were okay.

'Phew,' he muttered. 'That's better.'

'Feeling okay?' Orion asked. Steven nodded.

'I keep forgetting,' the cat went on. 'You get used to it after a while.'

'How do you stand it?' Steven asked. He knew he'd go mad if he had look at – whatever that was - for long.

'Oh, it's because I have a different kind of eyes to you,' Orion said, somewhat airily. 'You're not supposed to see like that, you see. You're not on that level.'

Steven waved at the air before his nose, almost expecting an explosion of colour. 'Is it – magic?'

Orion snorted. 'Magic! A very misunderstood word, in my experience. It's no more magic than I am.'

When he saw Steven staring at him, Orion huffed and went on, 'It's dream energy. This whole place is made from it. Dreamland, I mean. It's the same stuff that dreams are made out of, except on this level it has a concrete form.'

*Right...*

*Do I want to ask him what that means?*

Steven decided against it. There were an awful lot of questions he didn't know the answer to, and if he started asking then he'd never stop. He'd learn on the way. Yes, that was definitely a better option.

'Well,' Orion said, trotting down the hill, 'we can't stay here all day.'

Dutifully, Steven followed. He didn't have any idea where they were going, and that was actually a question he did want answered, but he didn't want to appear foolish by asking.

'Hey, where are we going?' he asked a minute later. It wasn't *that* foolish a question.

'We are going to find you a dream, ' the cat told him.

'A dream? Why?'

'Well, the Dream Thief is stealing dreams, yes?'

'Yes, I had heard that,' Steven replied testily.

'Then it follows that he'll go where the dreams are,' Orion said. 'Yes?'

'I suppose so,' Steven said, annoyed. He didn't like being talked down to at the best of times, and the fact that it was a cat doing it somehow made it worse.

'Trust me on this – it'll work a lot better if you do as I say, when I say it.'

'Fine,' Steven muttered, kicking a stone out of the way. 'You're the boss.'

'No, I'm your companion and helper,' Orion said. 'And if we work together, you should be just fine. Okay?'

'Fine, whatever you say,' Steven sighed.

'Good,' the cat said.

They had reached the bottom of the hill, and come onto a rough earthen track that wound down into a nearby valley. Orion began sniffing and pawing the earth.

*Is he looking for a dream or just scenting mice?*

'Is there one nearby, Mr Guardian?'

'Sssh,' Orion said. 'I'm trying to - '

'*What's that??*' Steven yelped suddenly.

A large, glowing ball of light, tinted coral-pink, was drifting up the path towards them. It was about the size of a football.

Orion sighed. 'That's a dream, Steven.'

'*That?* A dream?'

'Yes!'

'I didn't think they'd look like that,' Steven muttered.

'What did you think they'd look like? Did you think they would have a big sign hanging off them saying, 'I'm A Dream?' Anyway, we're lucky to find one so quickly.'

Orion trotted underneath it and looked up. 'It's a good sign, finding one this early. If you come here...'

Steven went closer. The dream seemed to sense his presence and came a little closer, the surface of the globe rippling warmly.

'What do I do?'

'You go in there,' Orion said.

'Go in there!' Steven laughed. 'It's tiny!'

There was no way he'd fit in there. He could barely fit his head in there as it was!

'No,' Orion said slowly, rolling his eyes in exasperation. 'It's a lot bigger when you get inside!'

'Oh,' Steven said, flushing. 'Okay then. What do I do? Just - '

'Actually, there's something you need to do first,' Orion said gently. He nodded at something over Steven's shoulder.

Steven looked behind him.

A squat pillar of dark metal had appeared by the side of the path.

'What's that?' Steven asked quietly. The sight of it gave Steven a creepy, itchy feeling along his back and arms. He knew, without knowing how he knew, that the metal would be cold to the touch.

'That,' Orion said slowly and carefully, 'is the Watchtower of Gorias.'

'What's it for?' Abruptly the day seemed colder, like a cloud had slid over the surface of the sun.

'It's for you, Steven,' Orion said.

'For me?'

'Before they can walk in the dreams of others, every Sleepwalker faces a test,' Orion said, sounding like he was reading from a manuscript. 'To tread the sleeping minds of those who dream is a grave responsibility. You must prove your worth before you can pass on.'

'Prove my worth?' Steven looked the dark box up and down. He was right – it gave off a chill, like an open refrigerator.

'You must enter, and return,' Orion said. 'I will wait for you here.'

'Can you tell me what's inside it?' Steven asked. The box seemed to be growing in size, stretching over him. Or was that his imagination?

'I cannot,' Orion said. 'That is for you alone.'

*Well, it seems like I don't have much choice.*

'There's no door,' Steven muttered.

'Touch the surface,' Orion said.

*Maybe I should have stayed in bed*, Steven thought glumly.

He placed a fingertip on the cold metal.

There was a slow, oily ripple, and –

A dark passageway.

Steven was becoming used to the strange shifts between here and there, the dissolve between one place and the next. It didn't hurt; he didn't even feel anything odd. There was only the sense that he had slipped into a deep pool of water.

The only difference was, anything could be in the water, lying in wait for him in the murky depths.

Anything at all.

The walls of the passage were of a rough dark brick, pitted and scarred as though they had been hacked out from the slag of a volcanic mountain. The ceiling was low over his head. On the nearest wall two fat sconces gave off a weak, sickly light. They wore thick cloaks of cobweb.

Steven could only see a few feet in front of him. Beyond the small patch of light, there was only darkness.

The rough stone floor was covered with a layer of dust an inch thick. It looked as if no-one had been here for a long time.

Steven scuffed his trainer back and forth, thinking. Small puffs of dust danced in the air like carefree ghosts.

If this was some sort of test, what was he supposed to do?

Absent-mindedly, he tapped the wall with his fingers. They met metal.

At the level of his eyes a plate of iron had appeared. It was about the size of a shoe-box, nailed crudely into the gritty mortar with peg-like bolts of steel. The surface was scratched and marred, as though something big had used it to sharpen its claws.

Steven tapped it cautiously.

Nothing happened.

He squinted in the bad light, trying to see if there was anything written on it.

Nothing.

*Well, that's strange.*

WHAT ARE YOU DOING HERE?

Steven started. The low, flat voice had come from all around him, as if the walls themselves had spoken.

WHAT ARE YOU DOING HERE?

It was totally without feeling. The sound of it settled a mantle of gloom about him.

'Who's-who's that?' Steven called out.

WHAT ARE YOU DOING HERE?

The mantle felt heavier, pressing down on him. Bracelets of lethargy encircled his arms, chains of weariness encased his ankles.

He needed to move. Whatever it was, it would drag him down if he stayed here.

Steven went down the passageway, away from the plate of iron, and the sconces over his head dimmed at the same time as two more brightened, further down. They showed him an identical patch of stone.

There was another plate of iron nailed to the wall.

His throat felt thick, clogged with dread. The lights went out behind him. Before him, beyond the small patch of illumination, there was only darkness.

Steven faced the iron plate. 'Who are you?'

YOU. It was said robotically. YOU. YOU.

'Where am I?' he asked.

HERE, it said. HERE...HERE...

Frightened, he began to walk forward, slowly at first and then faster and faster, and the passageway dimmed behind and brightened ahead, dimmed and brightened, dimmed and brightened.

Then he was running, pounding between the dark walls, feet thudding on the floor, and always the two fat sconces with cobwebs trailing beneath, and the hateful plate of iron.

*Stop!!*

Steven came to a halt, bending over, breathing heavily. *What is this place?*

Something rustled behind him, in the dark.

*What's that??!*

Between his shoulder-blades, a spot prickled. Someone - or something – was watching him, behind him, beyond the patch of light.

He strained to listen.

Nothing now. No sounds. The plate of iron gleamed blackly on the wall.

Carefully, moving as quietly as he could, Steven stepped forward, once, twice. As he put a foot down there seemed to be an echoing pace behind him, as though someone was trying to walk at exactly the same speed, matching their steps to his.

'Who's there?' he asked the plate of iron before he could help himself. That really scared him; seeing how close he was to panicking. He could see himself suddenly breaking into a terrified flight down the passageway, running and running through the same patch of light, with only the dimming and brightening of the sconces to mark his way.

THERE, the voice said. THERE...THERE...

*What to do? What to do??*

He didn't know. Steven chewed his lip nervously, looked down; stared in puzzlement at the ground.

There were footprints leading away into the next patch of light. Fresh footprints, clear through the layer of dust.

*Who made those?* Had someone been here before?

He looked behind. His own footprints receded back into the darkness.

*Who's here?*

He put his foot into the print.

It fitted exactly.

*How's that possible?*

Then he knew.

Suddenly, he laughed out loud, and it was like a beam of sunlight breaking through the dimness. He held his sides and laughed and laughed and laughed.

Steven had made the footprints himself. They were his. He'd been running in the same spot, all along the Watchtower, going round and round like a hamster on a wheel. The unknown someone he'd felt watching him – that was him too. He'd been watching himself, somehow, looking always forward in some kind of devilish loop.

He grinned at the iron plate. 'Got you. Didn't need anything else, did you? I scared myself.'

The walls trembled; the ceiling sighed. The cobwebs shook.

The plate of iron shuddered, and cracked down the centre.

The passageway collapsed.

One moment he was standing between the dark walls; the next he was back on the earthen path, the glowing dream drifting over his head.

Orion smiled. 'Nicely done, Sleepwalker.'

'Thanks,' Steven tried to appear unruffled, but his heart was still pounding, and his palms were damp. 'Nothing to it.'

'You have passed through the Watchtower and have proved your worth,' Orion went on, still sounding like he was reading from a scroll only he could see. 'You have earned passage through the Dreamland and the right to enter the dreams of others.

'Now...'

Steven turned to the brightly-shining orb of the dream. It was very close.

*Here we go!*

'Steven, wait!' Orion said urgently. 'First you must - '

Steven laughed. He'd just beaten the Watchtower – how hard could it be?

*It's only a dream!*

'No!' Orion cried.

Steven touched it.

For an instant, Steven had a glimpse of Orion's aghast face – lemon eyes wide, lips drawn back, whiskers arched – and then the landscape of the dream slid around him.

It was like an optician sliding a coloured lens before his eye. One moment there was nothing – the next, he *saw*.

He felt a flutter of apprehension and the thought that he might have just done something stupid – then he squashed it down. *It was only a dream, right?*

Steven stood on a narrow gravel path. On either side of him thick hedges rose above his head. A pungent scent was in the air, but he didn't recognise it.

*I suppose in a dream, it could be anything*, he thought.

Wondering where he was, Steven started down the path. From the sky above, it looked to be early afternoon, although he couldn't be sure.

The path went on for ten or fifteen feet before ending in an intersection. To the left and right, identical-looking paths led away.

Steven paused. *Where do I go?*

There were no signs, or anything to distinguish the two paths.

He tapped his finger against his lip a few times.

*I know!*

He was in a maze.

Well, there was only one thing to do – find the way out.

*Left or right?*

*Left*, he shrugged. He went down the left-hand path.

His trainers crunched over the white gravel, as if he were walking on broken glass.

After another ten feet or so there was an abrupt turn to the right, then another intersection.

*Right this time.*

Right again, at the next junction.

It was very quiet in the maze and after some time the minute grating of gravel began to tug at his nerves. The hedges were overgrown, the branches trailing on the path like wandering hands.

*I hope this isn't another test*, he thought, and laughed uneasily.

It sounded odd in the silence, and he coughed nervously.

The paths led on without end; left, right, left, left again in a dull, monotonous rhythm. Steven began to feel like a rat in laboratory, condemned to run endlessly round and round.

*This is just like the Watchtower!* he thought angrily. *This is supposed to be someone's dream! Who on earth dreamed this?*

Flustered, starting to pant with exertion and annoyance, he began to walk faster and faster. The paths twisted, branched, turned again and again. There was no sign of the exit.

At the next intersection he came to a halt.

*Let's think about this.*

He'd read something about mazes somewhere, something you did if you were lost.

*Something to do with your hands.*

What was it?

*Put your left hand out – no, right –*

*That was it!* If you needed to get out, you just had to put your hand on the nearest wall and follow it round. Then you'd find the exit.

*Okay then*. He put his right hand on the right-hand hedge. The leaves tickled his palm. Trotting, he began to follow the wall round.

Twilight had begun to fall, the light dimming. The sky was coloured with thick swirls of inky blue.

Left, right, a right again, left – left again, more left, more – right, right and – he was out! The hedges opened up before him and he came out onto a long driveway.

An enormous castle sat at the end. Ancient, weathered by time, the wind and rain, it thrust a central tower towards the sky. A huge wooden drawbridge was lowered, the entrance gaping like a throat.

Before it, blocking the way, was a swarming mass of thorns. Swollen, overgrown, they clung viciously together. They looked very sharp.

Steven grimaced as he saw it.

*Is there any chance I don't have to go through that?*

He turned and looked back at the maze.

It was a rough square of dull green, blunt and shambled, and beyond it were matted blocks of what must once have been gardens. In the far distance low hills formed a tight ring under the darkening sky.

*Can't believe I spent so long in there!*

There came a long, mournful breath of wind and with it a low, strange hooting that passed over the grounds of the castle and rustled the hedges of the maze, making the leaves whisper together as though confessing secrets. The hooting passed over the unkempt gardens and went on into the distance, echoing back from the basin of the hills.

Somehow, Steven knew he didn't want to linger. That sound had made him shiver.

He approached the thorn-bushes. They looked thick and spiky, twisted like the knots in a fishing-net.

*How am I supposed to - ?*

He had to get into the castle, that much was clear. Whatever he was here for waited within.

*How to get there, though?* The thorn-bushes had grown over the front of the castle and he didn't like to wander around as dark fell, searching for a way in.

Steven bent down low, peering at the ground. If the bushes didn't cluster too close there, maybe he could slide underneath...

The jagged thorns hung low, like greedy fingers waiting for the unwary.

*No chance. I'd be cut to ribbons trying to go through there.*

*If only I had a knife or something – or better yet a hedge-trimmer...*

Suddenly, his palms itched brightly, fiercely. He winced, bringing them up.

Nothing there.

Strange feeling. Like he'd been stung.

After a moment or two, it passed. He rubbed his palms on his jeans.

*Well, if there's no way through –*

A light blossomed high up in the tower, like a flare. It looked warm, rich, inviting.

The thorn bushes twisted and convulsed, rearing up as if someone was dragging them back. They looked unpleasantly like fat worms wriggling this way and that, and Steven stepped away as they trembled and shook and drew away from one another.

The path was clear. Steven went quickly down between them, ready to run if they looked like coming down again.

Then he was through and onto the vast drawbridge, moving swiftly over it, the old wood creaking and protesting under his feet –

- the swell of the archway opened onto a deserted courtyard, and keeping an eye on the warm spot of light above he entered the tower and climbed the grey steps of stone -

*Hang on! What just happened?*

He was almost at the top of the tower. Somehow he had passed from the entrance to the castle to here in a matter of moments. It had been smooth, seamless in fact.

*This is someone's dream. I can't forget that.*

*Musn't forget that.*

The light above him grew, becoming stronger and warmer, and he climbed faster and faster. A bright blue ball came bouncing down towards him, and he let it go, determined to reach the top. He had to see!

Then he was at the top of the tower.

A doorway opened onto a wide chamber richly decked in vermillion and ivory. In the centre was an enormous four-poster bed, with thick drapes let down on either side. A plush rug of ermine lay over the floorboards. A blazing fire burned in the hearth.

In one corner was a vast armoire. Thick, hooped dresses spilled out. Next to it stood a carved dressing-table, a lighted candle at either end. Creams and powders were before a gleaming mirror.

*Well, this isn't so bad*, Steven thought.

A point of light gleamed in the corner.

Squatting balefully in the shadows next to the hearth was an enormous spinning-wheel. Carved from some kind of black wood, it seemed to grin menacingly at him. A few threads of white silk hung from the spokes like the hair of a drowned sailor.

The wicked barb of the darning-needle jutted upwards like a scorpion's sting.

Steven recoiled. It was like a bloated spider, crooked and ugly. It seemed strange to see it in the midst of all the finery.

*Why would you want something like that around?*

Then a long, luxurious sigh rolled over the chamber.

There was someone in the bed.

*Who is that?!*

Steven hadn't realised someone was actually asleep in here. He hadn't thought about where the dreamer would be, and what it would be like to meet them face-to-face in their own dream.

And here they were. A tingling thrill ran like playful fingers over his skin.

Gently, he drew back the heavy drape.

Lying becalmed in the rumpled sheets, like an exotic creature cast up on some distant shore, there lay a girl. Her face was smooth and peaceful in sleep, her cheeks festooned with a bright smattering of freckles, and her long, lustrous hair trailed over the pillow like the fiery tail of a comet.

*Does she know I'm here?* Steven wondered.

She was murmuring softly to herself in slumber, but Steven couldn't quite make out the words. He wanted to lean in closer to hear what she was saying, but it felt strange. It would be invading her privacy, he recognised.

*Which is exactly what I'm doing already*, he thought ruefully.

She was quite beautiful, in a way.

*I wonder what colour her eyes are?*

*Wake her up and find out, then, idiot.*

Steven realised he was blushing and turned away, annoyed.

He took another look round at the chamber. It was bigger than he thought, huge, in fact, and suddenly he realised it was far too big to fit into the tower he'd seen from outside. It was more like the top floor of a house.

*I don't suppose that matters, though. I guess it must be whatever the dreamer wants it to be.*

His gaze roamed over the blazing fire and the overflowing armoire, and yet it kept coming back to rest on the menacing spinning-wheel and the wickedly bright needle.

Somehow the scene seemed familiar. He definitely felt like he'd seen it somewhere before. Yes, he had, in fact; the abandoned castle, the grounds gone wild, the thorn-bushes guarding the entrance...and now the girl asleep in her chamber, waiting for...

Waiting for what?

*I know this!*

Of course! It was one of the old stories, Snow White or Sleeping Beauty, a princess who fell under a wicked spell and slept for a hundred years. A princess who waited for her prince to come. A prince to kiss her and wake her from her enchanted slumber.

So the girl in bed was - dreaming of being a princess.

And he was...the prince?

*No, come on. I'm not the prince.*

The girl shifted in bed, murmuring louder.

*Am I supposed to...kiss her?*

Steven blushed again. He had kissed girls before, it wasn't that. He could remember – she was – it was –

With a sudden, slightly frightening jolt, as though he were sitting in a car that had just been rear-ended, Steven realised he couldn't actually remember. He couldn't remember the names of the girls he'd kissed, back in the real world. He couldn't remember much about them at all, in fact.

A knot of unease tightening in his stomach, he tried to think about the real world. How it felt to wake up in bed, get up and take a shower, eat his breakfast, walk to the park to mess around with his friends. Even go to school, of all things.

Anything.

He couldn't. It wasn't there, it had dwindled somehow, retreated away like a bashful suitor.

*This – this isn't right. Why can't I...*

A log cracked in the fireplace.

Steven blinked. A sudden urge to hurry came over him, driving all over thoughts out of his mind.

What was he doing standing around? He needed to do whatever it was he was here for and get out of here.

He crouched down by the side of the bed, whispering to the girl. 'Hey...I'm sorry, I'm not your prince or whatever. I can't kiss you, you see that, right? It'd be weird.'

The girl murmured again. She didn't look like she was waking up.

*Well, I can't leave her here. If she needs to be wake up, surely there's an easier way of doing it?*

Gently, he shook her by the shoulder. 'Hey there.'

Muttering irritably, she pulled away.

Steven tried again, a little more firmly. 'Hey.'

No response.

*She's really in a deep sleep.*

He leaned in closer. 'Hey, you need to wake up now. Come on! You want to stay here forever?'

The girl turned away from him, pushing herself deeper into the tangled mass of sheets.

*Not having much luck with this...*

*Oh well, here goes.*

Steven cupped his hands over his mouth. 'HEY!'

Her nose twitched as though a bee had settled there.

'HEY! HEY THERE! WAKE UP!'

The girl turned over again.

The bed, armoire, dressing-table, spinning-wheel – all vanished.

And they were falling.

Steven barely had time to gasp in astonishment before the raging wind ripped the breath from his throat.

They were plunging through the air. Hurtling down. Falling at a break-neck speed.

He could hear himself screaming, crying out desperately above the roar of the wind. Over and over he tumbled, spinning out of control, seeking to right himself as the earth and sky wheeled about him.

A mere foot or two away the girl fell with him. Her reddish hair streamed behind her. The white cotton of her nightdress flapped and billowed.

'Do something!' Steven shouted. 'This is your dream! Help us!'

She turned over lazily in the air and Steven caught a glimpse of her face.

*She was still asleep!!*

He didn't know whether to laugh or cry. This was – mad. *Mad!* They were going to die and she was still sleeping!

*Unless – this is still a dream. Right?*

*Right. Right!*

It must be one of those dreams. You fell and fell, but you woke up just before you hit the ground.

*Right?!*

He risked a glimpse down. A moan of horror escaped his lips.

They were heading for the centre of a wide field. The ground looked real. It looked hard.

*If this was her dream...*

She'll be fine! What about me?

He didn't know what happened to a Sleepwalker who got hurt in someone else's dream.

*And I don't want to.*

He thrust out his arm, trying to grasp her sleeve. She was too far away.

'Wake up!' he shouted, trying to make himself heard above the howl of the wind. 'Wake up! Please, you have to wake up!'

The girl's nose twitched again and then, infuriatingly, she *yawned!*

The ground was getting bigger. There was only a few moments left.

He stretched out his hand again, clawing for purchase. Her fingertip touched her sleeve, then slipped away.

*Too far!*

'Wake up,' Steven whispered. 'Come on. Wake up, or this is it...'

They went down.

The ground threw itself up to meet them.

Several things happened at once.

The girl opened her eyes. She saw the field. Then she saw Steven.

Caught on the knife-edge of the moment, he saw her eyes were a pearly grey.

Her mouth opened. 'Who - '

Then she winked out of the air and was gone.

Steven hit the ground.

He didn't smash into it. He didn't crumple, didn't fold up, wasn't pulverised.

He went *into* it.

It was like diving head-first into a lake of jelly.

*'Ah!'*

Then the dream popped like a bubble, and he was back in the Dreamland, standing on the path.

His arms and legs were trembling. His chest heaved up and down. His hands twitched and flexed.

Orion raised one eyebrow.

'Good trip?' he asked.

'...and then she just vanished,' Steven explained. 'She just disappeared right out of the air, and I hit the ground and nothing happened! I thought I was going to die!'

They were descending into a valley, bordered by thick gorse and fern. Sunlight was a balm on his skin after the terrifying plunge from the sky. It looked to be sometime in the afternoon; had been, in fact, since Steven had arrived in the Dreamland.

In the girl's dream it had been early evening, then twilight. Here, though, it seemed to be the same.

*I don't think Time changes here at all*, he thought.

Orion had been uncharacteristically silent while Steven was talking. Only once, when Steven told him how his hands had itched when wishing for something to cut through the tangled bushes, had he said something under his breath.

'Were you frightened?' he asked Steven now.

What a strange question. Of course he had been frightened!

'Well, yes,' Steven considered. I was scared when I was falling, even though it was just a dream. I believed it, though. Who wouldn't have been?'

'No, not then,' Orion said softly. 'When you were in the chamber, trying to wake up the dreamer.'

Steven thought about it. It was definitely strange, and being outside the maze and hearing that eerie hooting sound had been unsettling, but once he was in the tower, he wasn't frightened then. It had been a relief to get inside, in fact.

'No, I wasn't,' he answered. 'Being inside someone else's dream was weird, yeah, but I wasn't frightened then. I suppose you're going to tell me I should have been scared, right?'

Orion said nothing.

'It's a dream, though,' Steven said, after a moment or two. 'Just one of those falling ones. Everyone has them! Something happens in a dream and you just – wake up! Like she did!'

Orion was silent.

'Well, are you going to say anything?' Steven snapped in frustration. 'You've got a real way about you, you know that? Okay, okay, you know everything and I know nothing, is that what you want to hear?'

Orion stopped walking. His whiskers twitched.

'Steven,' he said, 'sit down for a moment.'

Steven cast about for a suitable seat and, finding none, he crouched somewhat awkwardly on the ground.

*This doesn't sound good*, he thought. It was the same tone of voice his Mum and Dad used when telling him off.

The pupils of Orion's eyes were as black as onyx. It was deeply unnerving. Even though Steven towered over the cat, he felt a sudden prickling along the back of his neck, as though he were standing next to a generator capable of immense force and power.

'Steven,' Orion went on quietly, 'I have to tell you that you were in great danger in there. I tried to stop you before you went in, but you ran ahead without listening to me. You should have waited.'

Steven flushed, cheeks burning crimson. 'What – what do you mean? I was fine! Nothing was going to go wrong! It's -'

' – only a dream?' Orion interrupted. 'In your world, yes. Here, it's different. Very different.'

'I-,' Steven began to bluster, then stopped. He knew Orion was right. He *had* raced ahead without thinking.

He'd thought, *what was so scary about a dream, anyway?*

He'd ignored Orion's warning and gone straight in.

An image appeared in his mind of a dark room strewn with mouse-traps primed to catch the unwary; every step must be carefully placed. One wrong move, and - *snap!*

'Here in the Dreamland,' Orion went on, 'there is, like your world, much that is good and glorious and right. Also like your world, there is much that is dark and dangerous, and hurtful if you do not know what you are about.

'You must tread carefully, Steven. You are a Sleepwalker, one who can enter the dreams of others. Few now have that power. It is a great privilege, and an important one.

'It was not always so. Once there were many such as yourself, coming and going through the halls of slumber, keeping watch over the land.

'That was a grand time, Steven. There is a place which marks all those who have gone before you, and one day I will show it to you. Not today. Today you must learn the one rule, the only rule, of being a Sleepwalker.

'You must never wake a dreamer up when you are inside a dream. Never. Your life, and possibly the life of the dreamer, depends on it. To do so could possibly tear everything apart.

'A dreamer is always in their own dream; they might seem awake, asleep, or come as an animal or an object. They may even be invisible, but they are always there.

'They may talk with you, play with you, even fight with you. Whatever it is, the rule is always the same. *Never wake them up.*'

Steven's mouth was dry. He'd – he'd tried to wake that girl up! He'd grabbed her shoulder, even shouted at her!

'What – what happens if I do?' he asked fearfully. 'Would everything - '

'Have you ever been woken up suddenly, whilst you were dreaming?' Orion asked gravely. 'How did it feel?'

He had been. It felt awful; disorientating, painful almost. 'Yeah. I didn't like it.'

Orion said, 'Now imagine being woken up inside your dream, while you're still sleeping, by someone who shouldn't be there in the first place, who has just walked into your dream and pulled it apart.'

Steven looked away, across to the horizon. Even in the afternoon's hazy light he could see the far-off mountains and their light caps of snow. They looked remote, vast, forbidding.

Without warning a great tearing loneliness swelled up within him, a wave of fear and doubt and loneliness that felt as if it would sweep him away. He could have woken the dreamer up, ripped her peaceful slumber to shreds.

How close to he had come, without knowing, to disaster.

*What is this? What am I doing here?*

This wasn't his place. He didn't belong here. He came from the waking world. Football in the park, cartoons on the TV. Normal life. Every-day life. Happy. Dull. Safe.

Yet here he was, in this strange, frightening place where animals talked and a vision waited around every corner.

His shoulders slumped.

*What to do?*

Could he go on?

Did he even want to?

He hung teetering on the edge, and a memory fluttered like a butterfly at the edge of his mind: the sundered thread of his own dream, the remnants of his imagination hanging limp and tattered, paining him like a broken limb.

There was someone out there, taking dreams, stealing them away. He had, unwittingly, come to the brink of misfortune; yet another courted it deliberately, taking that which rightfully belonged to the dreamer.

The Dream Thief.

It had happened to him, and it had happened to others too.

Having understood the damage he had almost done, he could not, would not, let another do so.

Her eyes had been pearly grey.

Yes. Yes, I will.

Steven took a deep, shuddering breath.

'Okay?' Orion asked gently. Steven nodded.

'The Dream Thief, whoever he is,' he said, getting to his feet, 'what does he want the dreams for? What does he do with them?'

'I'm not sure,' Orion admitted, 'but you can be certain that whatever he's doing, it'll have grave consequences for us.'

'Do you know where he is now?' Steven asked. 'I don't want to run in to him round the next corner.'

'It's okay,' Orion nodded confidently. 'He's far away from here.'

Suddenly, borne towards him on the wind, Steven heard a burst of music that brought a broad smile to his face.

*I know that!*

'Where's that coming from?'

'Well, you've been through a lot in quite a short time,' Orion said, 'so I thought you could do with a break.'

They had come to the end of the valley. The music rang out again, and with a rush of delight    Steven knew what it was.

*A calliope!*

It was a fair.

And what a fair!

There was an enormous red-and-white-striped Big Top, from which Steven could hear deafening roars and cheers; a looping, swirling rollercoaster; a sedately gliding Ride-the-Teacups stand, a mess of crashing, hooting Bumper-Cars; a spooky-looking Funhouse with a clown's face manically grinning over the doorway; Hook-the-Duck stalls, Shoot-the-Target-stalls, Dunk-the-Fool in the water stalls. The crisp smell of candyfloss was in the air, mingled with fries roasting in oil, tangy vinegar and sober salt.

And here and there wisps of a deeper, more exotic scent.

Steven began to scamper away, then sheepishly turned back.

Orion nodded, smiling a little. 'It's alright. Have a look around. I'll come and find you in a little while.'

Steven grinned impishly back and ran off, diving into the crowd.

'Not too long, mind!' Orion called from over his head - but he was already lost in wonder, trying to look in every direction at once.

He hadn't been to a fair in years! He wanted to try everything, go on every ride. He didn't have any money, but that didn't matter as everything seemed to be free - a turn on the Shoot-the-Duck stall netted him a large fluffy rabbit, which he gave away, laughing; he missed all the rings on the Hook-a-Duck stall and gave it up as a lost cause, laughing still.

*Sometimes the Dreamland wasn't so bad*, he thought to himself, watching the rollercoaster twisting above his head.

'Wonder if there's time to go on that?' he murmured.

'Step right up, ladies and gents! Find out the power of your arm! This way, ladies and gentlemen!'

Nearby a round-faced, jolly-looking man held a large wooden mallet up before him. He had a Test-Your-Strength pole, the large red bell at the top waiting whoever was strong enough to make it ring.

Steven went over, squeezing his way to the front. The big man examined the crowd, smiling cheerfully. 'Who's going to be first? Young sir, how about you?'

He offered the mallet to Steven, who grinned sheepishly and shook his head. He'd never have the strength to reach the bell. He'd never seen it done before, either.

'Who will be first?' the man called, offering the mallet out again.

With a deep grunt, a huge man shouldered his way forward.

Steven's mouth dropped open.

His shoulders were as wide as a door-frame, and humped hillocks of muscle bulged from his chest and arms. His top half was human, but beneath the waist he had grey-furred legs with hooves for feet. From his thick neck a bull's head rose, curved yellow horns protruding behind his tiny ears.

*A bull's head. He has a bull's head.*

The man – if that was what he was – snorted air out of his snub, pinkish nose.

*He has a gold ring in there*, Steven thought. *A gold ring.*

He felt like something had come loose inside him for a moment and was whirling round and round hysterically. For a moment he thought he would faint, or burst out laughing.

The man held out a heavy, shovel-sized hand for the mallet. The stall owner, chuckling as though he met bull-headed men every day, handed it over.

The bull-head man hefted it casually. It looked like a twig in his meaty hand.

He stepped in front of the plate and raised the mallet high.

There was a murmur of anticipation, then –

'GRAAAAR!'

He brought the mallet crashing down.

It smashed into the plate. The bell didn't just ring – it flew off the top of the pole and smacked into the ground by Steven's foot.

The stall owner chuckled again. The bull-head man lowered the mallet, staring at it with an air of bafflement. Steven noticed that his eyes were small and quite close together.

'Well done, sir!' the owner cried, clapping his hands. 'A mighty stroke.'

The bull-headed man looked about slowly. 'Graaaar?'

Very gently, the owner took the mallet away. The bull-headed man blinked at his empty palm for a moment, then stomped off between the tents.

Steven let out a long breath. He watched the man's bulging shoulders flex as he walked away.

He had a name. Something out of an old legend...

*The Minotaur! That was it!*

Steven took a closer look at the crowd. He'd been so caught up in the sights and sounds of the fair he hadn't realised it was the first time he'd seen a crowd of people in the Dreamland. Everyone seemed normal; mothers and fathers leading small children by the hand; small huddles of teenagers pretending they'd seen it all before; courting couples linking arms as they strolled through the stalls.

The only thing out of the ordinary was that everyone wore a slightly blank expression, as if they were perpetually thinking about something else. Every now and again someone would shake their heads, as though coming out of a daze, and for a moment or two look around in puzzlement; then they would look blank again.

*No-one's truly here*, Steven thought. *Everyone's asleep.*

*There!*

As though they had been called by his attention, he began to see odd figures in the crowd.

Next to the Bumper-Cars a little girl with golden hair stood sucking her thumb with a tattered teddy-bear in one hand. A few paces away a haggard old woman stood clutching a broomstick. She wore a tattered black dress and a broad black hat that came to a point over her head, and her beady eyes gleamed menacingly.

*Ugh. I suppose she's a witch, then.*

A stiff-looking man in a pin-striped three-piece suit went stomping past, clenching a briefcase in one hand and a rolled-up newspaper in the other. He had a neatly-trimmed moustache above his pursed lips. As Steven watched he walked past a woman with long dark hair and a blouse made of what looked like seashells. She was soaking wet, and had seaweed draped over her shoulders. Looking at her feet, Steven saw to his shock that she had a large emerald tail below the waist, flapping on the ground.

She was a mermaid.

The stern-looking man walked by without looking twice.

Steven shook his head in amazement.

*That's the Dreamland*, he thought to himself.

He brought some candyfloss from a nearby stall and wandered around. He wasn't sure what to do now. He'd been on most of the rides, and seeing the Minotaur had brought him out of his carefree mood. He had remembered where he was, and why.

He found himself in front of the Funhouse. The clown's face over the doorway was unpleasant. The artist had done a good job; the bright red lips were wide and full, stretched back in a twisted smile, and the eyes were bright and glittering. The whiteness of the face made him uneasy. It reminded him of -

'Going in, young sir?'

The voice made him blink.

By his elbow, a colourfully-dressed man had appeared. His tunic and leggings were of purple and green, with ruffles of orange at his wrists and ankles. Wreaths of chestnut hair tumbled to his shoulders, and he wore elegant shoes of velvet topped with a silver buckle.

'Er – no,' Steven said. 'It's not my sort of thing, really.'

'Ah, 'tis a pity!' the man declared, producing a deck of cards from thin air and shuffling them. 'No harm in a little fright now, is there? Well, pick a card, sir, any card!'

Steven looked at them. The man seemed friendly. 'Well, alright. This one!'

He tucked it behind his hands and took a peek.

The Ace of Spades.

Making sure the man couldn't see it, he handed it back.

The cards blurred as he shuffled the pack again. Then he *ummed* and *aahed* for a few moments,  before plucking one out and holding it up in front of Steven's face.

'Is this your card?'

The Ace of Spades.

'That's right!' Steven said. The man giggled.

'You lose, young sir!' The man tucked the pack of cards away somewhere and executed an extravagant bow, leaning over his left leg with his arm outstretched. 'Allow me to introduce myself. My name is Lokin, resident conjurer, magician and all-round purveyor of tricks and artifices. And you are - ?'

'Steven. My name's Steven.' He wasn't altogether sure what to make of Lokin; he was a bit odd.

*Mind you, a bit odd is probably normal, here.*

'Pleased to meet you, indeed,' Lokin said. 'Ah, but where are my manners? Is it not your custom to shake hands upon being introduced?'

He held out one hand. Steven took it.

'*Ow!*'

There was a sharp pain in his hand and Steven wrenched his arm back. In the centre of his palm a crimson dot of blood had appeared.

'Hey, that's not funny!' he snapped angrily.

Lokin giggled again, revealing something like an old-fashioned joy buzzer in his hand. Instead of a buzzer, there was a pin in the centre. 'Forgive me, young sir. A small joke. No harm meant, of course. Yes?'

'Okay, I suppose,' Steven muttered resentfully, rubbing his hand. He wasn't sure he liked the strange man; that was a cruel trick to play.

'Well, I must be away,' Lokin said. 'I do recommend trying the Funhouse, if you have the time. There's all sorts in there.

'But before I go, let me present you with my card.' He whipped one out from thin air and presented it to Steven.

It was like a Joker card from a normal pack, except there was a picture of Lokin in the middle instead. As Steven glanced at it his picture winked, then turned stood on his head.

'That's – nice,' he muttered.

The picture-Lokin began to juggle, and he tucked the card away in his back pocket.

'Now you have a little piece of me wherever you go,' Lokin said. 'Farewell, young sir!'
He sprang lithely away. 'Until we meet again!'

'Yeah, sure,' Steven said. His hand was still bleeding, and he wiped it on the ground.
As he straightened up, he saw someone watching him.

Some distance away, beneath a line of trees at the meadow's edge, a tall figure stood. Swathed and hooded in a mottled green robe, Steven had only the faintest impression of a fierce, high-boned face, and the brush of the figure's gaze.

Even as he watched, the figure melted slowly away into the trees and vanished from his sight.

*Is that - ?*

Steven went to go after him, then stopped. It couldn't be the Dream Thief, could it?

Orion said he was far away. Besides, there were so many odd characters around here, who knew who the figure was or what he wanted.

But why was he so interested in Steven? If it had been the Dream Thief, surely he would have done something?

He shook his head. Whoever it was had gone anyway. *Strange.*

A sound from a nearby tent caught his attention. It sounded like a collective gasp, as though many voices had suddenly drawn breath in unison. It had come from a large purple tent Steven hadn't noticed earlier.

He went over. The tent was covered in drawings and symbols that he didn't recognise; circles with lines through the centre, loops and whirls that could have been words in a different language.

Had he seen something like that before? Written on a door somewhere?

The memory refused to come and he bent over and lifted the tent-flap, peering within.

The tent was larger inside than he expected and very warm. Two enormous braziers stood at the back, giving forth streaks of light that wavered on the canvas walls as though he was looking into a vast aquarium. An exotic scent permeated the air, and Steven recognised it as the source of the strange smell he'd noticed when arriving at the fair.

Between the two smoking braziers stood a man in a white, shapeless robe. Streaks of paint lined his cheeks and forehead like the claw-marks of a savage bird. Lined and seamed, his skin was like the bark of an ancient tree, weathered with the years yet strong enough to withstand the harshest wind.

A semi-circle of children were seated before him. Perched on plump cushions and low stools, they gazed raptly up at the old man.

Steven, feeling like he had intruded on something secret, began to back out of the tent.

Seeing him peering in at the scene, the man raised his head. 'Steven. Come in.'

*How does he know my name? Everyone here knows my name!!*

Steven ducked inside, letting the tent-flap drop down behind him. A girl with curly brown ringlets shuffled to one side, and he took a seat in the semi-circle.

'You've travelled far,' said the old man.

'You know my name,' Steven said, 'but who are you?'

The man smiled, and as he did so his face lost its aura of sternness and became kindly and warm. 'I have many names, but you may call me Homer.'

A small bleary-eyed boy tugged at his man's robe.

'Story!' he said. 'We want story!'

A chorus of agreement rose up from the gathered children.

'Oh, very well,' Homer said amicably. 'You shall have a story indeed.

'Are you sitting comfortably?'

There was a chorus of nodding heads and *yeses*. Steven settled himself more comfortably. It reminded him curiously of school as a young boy, where everyone gathered on the carpet to listen to Teacher reading.

Homer tucked his fingers under his chin and peered around, making sure everyone was listening. The light made caverns from his eyes and the furrows of his cheeks, mountains from his forehead and jaw.

'Once upon a time, the Dreamland was all in darkness. It was not even called the Dreamland then. No foot walked the earth, no deer ran in the forest, no fish swam in the seas. There was only emptiness, and silence.

'Then, one day, the Power arose. It shone like a torch from the heavens, lighting up the land, the sky, the ocean. It brought forth the first people, men and women, boy and girls. The animals, the birds, the fish. All manner of things.

'And with the living beings came the dreams. The first dreams.

'Rough and crude, the first dreams were. Darkness and light, for the most part, with little enough in-between. It was the beginning.

'Yet as the men and woman grew stronger, grew to know the land and themselves, so too did the dreams grow stronger, brighter, fiercer. Spoke they did of their dreams, and the world, and how they came to be.

'And the dreams were seen for themselves, bound to their dreamers. The two, together, for all Time. Never to be torn asunder.'

The braziers guttered and flamed. No-one in the circle moved, or spoke.

'And with the knowing came the chance of un-knowing, and un-making; and in that instant the Balance was decreed, the Balance that will hold until the end of all things. And the Three came to be, charged with its keeping.

'Three they were, three there are, and three there will always be. The Maiden, the Earl, and the Lord.'

Steven remembered the silver-haired lady on her high throne; the man with his robe of many colours; the figure in black, shrouded in shadow.

'The Maiden of Sleep, who brings rest to all who weary and falter. The Earl of Dreams, who has charge over the imaginings of all. The Lord of Nightmares, who rules the night-time terrors, and seeks to bend all to his will.

'One for the light,' Homer said. 'One for the dark. And one to keep the Balance.

'So it was; so it is; so it shall be, until the end of Time.'

'The end.'

Homer shifted, stretched his legs and sighed; and the story was over.

A few of the children clapped, or laughed; a few went *awwwww*.

A long, low breeze swept through the tent. There came a shifting in the air, a changing; a few of the children vanished and others took their place, blinking and yawning, looking around curiously. The girl next to Steven disappeared, and he found himself sitting next to a tall girl with straw-blond hair who looked bemused to find herself there.

'Some wake,' Homer said. 'Others sleep; some dream. So it goes.'

Slowly, Steven got up. The heat was making him dizzy; he felt light-headed, like he might faint.

'Excuse me – I need to - '

Homer nodded, and pressed his palms together in front of his face in a curious gesture.

'Until we meet again, Steven.'

Walking a little unsteadily, Steven made his way outside and stood blinking in the sunshine.

After a moment or two he felt better. It was good to be in the fresh air. Listening to Homer had been hypnotic; he felt himself going into a trance, lulled by the power of the story.

Now he knew who the three figures in the throne-room were, and what they stood for. The Maiden and the Earl were friendly, that he could sense, whereas the Lord -

He was glad he hadn't seen much of the Lord.

Despite the warmth of the afternoon, he shivered.

'Ah, there you are!' Orion came trotting up.

'Hi,' Steven said. 'Did you have fun?'

Orion looked mildly affronted, as though fun was far too undignified a prospect. 'Actually, I've been looking up a few old friends, Steven.

'And I see you've been visiting with our resident story-teller. Did you learn anything?'

Steven told him what Homer had said, but Orion sniffed dismissively.

'I've heard it before. Come, we need to moving on.'

Sighing, Steven followed. They made their way to the edge of the fair, following a path into the forest. Steven thought about telling Orion about Lokin, and the strange figure in the mottled green robe, but he was annoyed the cat wasn't interested in Homer's story.

*Serves him right if I don't tell him*, he thought.

As they passed beneath the shadow of the trees Steven looked back at the fair.

The rollercoaster was looping up and down and he could hear distant screams and shouts of joy. Above the heads of the crowd he could see the Minotaur's peaked horns moving away between the tents.

'Orion - '

He stopped.

Floating through the trees, riding the breeze like a galleon in full sail, came a dream.

Like a lantern bobbing on a string, the dream hung in the air before him, driving all thought from his mind. It was...beautiful...so beautiful...

'A-ha!' Orion cried. 'This is another chance, Steven. You must become accustomed to walking in dreams. Hey, don't touch it yet!'

Steven pulled his fingers back. 'I wasn't going to!' he protested. It just looked so warm, so shiny...

'When you're in there, there's something I want you to practice,' Orion told him. 'Come over here for a moment.'

Unwillingly, Steven moved away from the floating dream. He found it hard to look away; the glowing sphere rested almost patiently on the breeze, rising and falling with each gentle puff of wind.

It looks like a jellyfish, he thought. Or like a bird, something like that...

'Steven!'

'Ouch!' Steven rubbed his ankle.

'Pay attention!' Orion peered up at him. 'This is important. You remember when you had an itch in your hands, when you were trying to find something to cut the thorn-bushes with?'

Steven nodded. It had been an odd feeling, like his palms were suddenly heating up. It wasn't painful, it was more a sense of - *expectation*, like something was coming, or - *arriving*, somehow.

'You can Summon things, Steven!' Orion said excitedly. 'Sleepwalkers can do that, in dreams. It's part of your power. You can imagine something before you, like a pair of shears in that particular dream, and then – in an instant! – it's there for you.'

'Wow,' Steven said, impressed. That sounded pretty good. 'What kind of things? Like a car? Or a gun or something? Anything at all?'

Orion frowned. 'No, nothing like that. Why are you humans all so fierce?'

He went on, 'It's only something that would help you at that precise point in time. Then and only then. You can't Summon just anything you want. That's the way it works.'

'Okay,' Steven said. 'So when I was lost in the maze, I could Summon a – compass, or something like that? A map?'

'Yes,' Orion nodded vigorously. 'Just so! It's a skill that needs getting used to, and practicing, of course.

'Now go ahead.'

He motioned towards the hovering dream. Steven got to his feet and approached.

He felt its warmth, its welcome, over his face and arms.

Slowly, he lifted one finger and touched it.

It folded around him noiselessly.

Whereas the first dream had slid smoothly into place like a well-oiled bolt, this one gently wrapped itself around him like a blanket.

He saw the forest, the path, Orion –

- then a slow mixing of scenes, like oil and water pouring through his vision –

- and he was sitting beneath an enormous tree, cross-legged, in the cool shade of a long leafy limb.

The tree was in the centre of a verdant meadow and he caught the sweet scent of honeysuckle and foxgloves. Behind him, a stream gurgled happily away into the distance. The sun blazed overhead.

Steven sighed with pleasure. He felt unutterably peaceful, at ease with himself and the world.

The sky was a pure azure, mantled with the merest wisp of cloud.

Idly, he watched the wind toy with the luxurious grass, brushing it back and forth like a child at play. A flash of brown fur caught his eye, and he sat up to see if he could catch a glimpse of whatever it was.

A long brown ear vanished into the emerald sheaves.

*A hare*, he thought, settling back down. *That was a hare.*

There was a soft hooting from the branches above his head, and he saw a long-winded shadow take off from the branches of the tree and take flight over the meadow.

*An owl*, he thought.

He'd read somewhere that owls didn't come out during the day. What did it matter? Here anything was possible. His thoughts had a slow, rich, honeyed drip, and he floated amongst them as though submerged in a pool of warm water.

Close by bees were droning, moving this way and that amongst the flowers, and Steven leaned back against the solid oak behind. Its weight and firmness were comforting, reassuring.

*There are lots of trees here*, he thought drowsily. *Why aren't there as many at home?*

*When I get back, I'll plant a lot of trees.*

*When I get back...*

He realised that, as before, he could remember nothing of what it felt like to be in the waking world. He knew who he was, but beyond that -

He tried to follow the thought to its natural conclusion, but it slipped away from him, spiralling away like a rock dropped into the ocean.

*Why bother?* he thought.

The wind sighed and murmured.

*I could stay here forever*, he thought.

The sunlight wove timeless patterns on the grass.

Absently, he scratched his ankle where Orion had prodded him.

*What did he say? Practice?*

*Practice what?*

There was nothing to do; nothing that needed to be done.

He stretched his arms up above his head. The leaves above him whispered as though sharing secrets.

*Something else Orion had said...the rule?*

*Oh yes. The rule. Never wake up the dreamer.*

He tried to spot the dreamer, wherever they might be. There was only the sun-drenched meadow, the dappled tree.

*Could it be the hare? Or the owl? Maybe one of the two.*

That would be good, to dream of being a hare.

There was a warm breath of wind and over the meadow came a butterfly, iridescent blue and green, gold flecking its tiny body. Wings swelling to the current, it hovered inquisitively before Steven.

He held out a hand.

The butterfly fluttered above it, settled gently down.

He looked at it closely. It was beautiful.

'Hello,' he whispered. The butterfly beat its wings softly.

Steven held it close to his eye. 'Who are you? Are you the dreamer?'

The butterfly made no sound.

*This could be the dreamer*, he thought.

*If it is...*

*Is he a butterfly for real, then? Or she?*

*Are you what you dream while you're dreaming it?*

The meadow, the laughing brook – at this moment, there was nothing else. The dreamer was that which they dreamed they were, and nothing else.

*Is he still a man, or a woman, and a butterfly at the same time? Which one is he really?*

Suddenly, unable to help himself, he coughed. The butterfly took fright and sprang deftly away.

*If he's dreaming he's a butterfly – is he someone dreaming they're a butterfly, or a butterfly –*

He couldn't hold on to it. It slid away, slipped through his fingers.

He tried again, concentrating hard.

*If you were the dreamer, and were in your own dream – you could be anything, really. A boy, a girl, a dog – a cat, even...*

*I wonder what Orion dreams? Does he even dream at all?*

*Do people here dream?*

Steven looked up at the sky.

*I'm in the dream too. And I'm not the dreamer.*

*Am I part of the dreamer, then? Am I part of the dream?*

*How do I know?*

*How do I know what's real and what isn't?*

*How do I know what I am?*

He said it out loud, frowning, struggling to give voice to it. 'I am...Steven...'

'I am...Steven...I am...'

'I am...'

Gently, he closed his hand over the spot where the butterfly had settled.

The sun beamed down on the meadow. The grass whispered. The stream chattered and babbled.

As softly as a page being turned, the dream changed.

He was standing in a forest clearing.

In the centre was a pool with water as clear as crystal. Rocks clustered on the bank. He heard the slap and splash of something breaking the surface.

It must have been midday in the meadow, underneath the tree; now it was early evening. The sun was starting to go, flinging strips of gold across the forest, and the sky was turning to cobalt as though someone had spilled an inkwell across the horizon.

A young boy was perched on a rock by the pool, holding a fishing rod. He wore a wrinkled grey T-shirt with a picture of a beach on it and tattered shorts. His sandals were on the rock behind him, and his feet were dangling in the water.

Steven had come back to himself as the dream changed. He felt an odd, drifting feeling as the landscape shifted around him and a strange wistfulness, as though he had dozed off in the garden on a summer's afternoon.

He went to the pool. It was bursting with fish, their scales flashing and shimmering, miniature rainbows dancing in an underwater kingdom.

The boy noticed him and smiled. 'Hello.'

'Hello,' Steven replied carefully. He wasn't sure what the boy would do. Orion's warning was at the back of his mind. *Never wake up the dreamer*.

The boy didn't seem put out by his presence. 'Are you here to fish?'

'No,' Steven said. 'I'm here to...'

*What to say? I'm a Sleepwalker, and I like walking into other people's dreams? I'm here to practice Summoning objects out of thin air, apparently?*

'...to look around,' he finished lamely.

'Oh,' the boy said blankly, as though the idea of someone not wanting to fish was hard to grasp. 'Well, that's good, I suppose. It's a shame you don't like fishing. This is the best place.'

Suddenly, the rod tensed in his hands and he gave a whoop of delight.

Bracing himself against the rock, digging his toes into the bank, he hauled back on the line. 'Here we go!'

There was a splash and a huge silver fish appeared at the end of the boy's line, twisting and thrashing.

'Wow!' the boy exclaimed. 'Look at that! It's a beauty!'

Steven grinned. The delight on the boy's face was infectious. 'It's certainly big. Well done!'

'Thanks!' the boy puffed. Heaving the fish onto dry land, he grasped it firmly with both hands. It twitched and gasped, throwing off beads of shining water that spattered on the rocks.

'Do you catch many fish here?' Steven asked. He wanted to ask the boy about his dream, but he knew he couldn't do that. To the dreamer, the dream was real as normal life: and to ask questions about it would be to mark himself out as a stranger, as if he were an alien landing on Earth for the first time and seeking answers.

*Until I know a bit more about being a Sleepwalker, anyway.*

'Well, yes and no,' the boy replied. His blonde hair was damp at the front and his front two teeth were slightly crooked, which gave his smile an endearing quality. 'It depends on the day. Sometimes the fish aren't interested. Today, they want to play!'

Moving with a great deal of skill for one so young, he slid the hook out of the fish's gums and, taking hold of it once more, slipped it back into the pool.

The fish flicked its tail and then slid to the bottom of the water, looking none the worse for wear.

Whistling, the boy sent the line snapping back in.

Steven left him to it. He wanted to have a look around the clearing. How big was the dream? How far did the forest go back? If he walked into it, could he just keep on going?

As he advanced between the trees he could hear tiny rustles all around that told him animals were on the move, although he couldn't see any.

*Probably frightened them away.*

There didn't seem to be anyone else here, either. It was just him and the boy.

He ducked under a low-hanging branch. It did seem to go on -

'Ow!'

Rubbing his nose, Steven stepped back a few paces.

He'd run straight into an invisible barrier. Exploring left and right, he discovered it stretched away on both sides, as smooth – and as transparent – as glass.

He put his hand on it, as he had done in the maze, and walked around the clearing.

It was the same all around. The barrier sprang up roughly the same distance into the tree-line, and there were no gaps where Steven could pass through. While the forest itself seemed to go on and on, there was no way to go far from the clearing itself.

The pool, and the boy fishing, was the heart of it.

Dreams, it seemed, had limits.

*Limits because they're dreams, or because of the imagination of the dreamer?*

A question for another time.

*I've got a lot of questions. Maybe I need to write some of them down...if I had anything to write with...*

He went back to the pool. The boy was still on the rock.

He looked up as Steven approached. 'Oh, hello.'

'Hello,' Steven said.

'Are you here to fish?' he asked.

'Er...'

*Doesn't he remember me?*

'I was here just a minute ago.'

'Oh,' the boy said blankly. 'Um...do you want to fish?'

It seemed their conversation had limited potential. Even though Steven had just spoken to him, the boy clearly didn't remember him or what they talked about.

Since it was the boy's dream and he was focused on fishing, that was the only thing that mattered. Anything else didn't seem to make an impression. Steven wasn't sure whether it was funny or annoying.

*Still, while I'm here...*

'Yes,' Steven answered. 'I'll give it a try.'

The boy beamed in delight. 'Great!'

He patted the rock next to him.

Steven sat down. The rock was warm and smooth and, following the boy's example, he took off his trainers and socks and slipped his feet into the water.

He sighed with pleasure. The water was deliciously cool and he felt it trickling between his toes.

*When did I sit down last?*

He couldn't remember.

'Where's your rod?' the boy asked.

Steven looked up. 'Hmmm?'

'You need a rod if you want to fish!' the boy exclaimed. 'Where's yours?'

'Umm...' Steven said, trying to think.

*Good point...*

The boy sighed. 'You can't *fish* without a *rod*. Everyone knows *that*.'

Steven fought the sudden urge to dunk the boy's head underwater in the pool and thought about it.

Orion said he could Summon things in a dream: things he needed at that point in time.

Well, right now he needed a fishing rod.

Steven flexed his hands, looking at the palms, the lines on them crinkling in the fading light. Life line, love line -

*- the itching, flaring feeling, the sense of arriving –*

He could do it now. He'd get a rod. Somehow.

Steven closed his eyes. In his mind he tried to see a fishing rod, to sense the weight and heft and shape of it, to hold it in his imagination as he sought to hold it in his hands –

*What's a fishing rod? It's long, and made of metal...it bends, like a willow branch...there's a hook on the end, a wheel for winding in...*

'Ah!' A sudden jolt down his arms. As if an electric current had shot through them.

The boy tutted. 'You're disturbing the fish.'

Steven ignored him, thinking hard. He could see the shape of the rod clearly now, a heavy presence behind his closed eyes. He needed to make the jump from *in there* to *out here*.

How would it feel?

*Smooth to the touch...his hands could fit round it easily...heavy, but not too heavy...he could lift it...*

Again the sudden jolt down his arms, flowing quick and hot. His hands pulsed with force, the air between them crackling and vibrating.

*Here – it's here!*

*A fishing rod was – a fishing rod is –*

*Here!*

A sharp crack like a snapping branch - a flare of light - and then it was in his hands, real and solid. There came the soft dunk of water as the hook dropped into the pool.

'Yeah!' the boy cried.

Slowly, Steven opened one eye. His arms were thrumming, his palms hot as if he'd put them close to a fire –

- and he held a silver fishing rod in his hands.

Steven laughed out loud. He'd done it!

Until the rod had appeared in his hands Steven hadn't completely believed it would work.

He looked the rod up and down, admiring how the light slid over the polished silver of the shaft.

*Not bad*, he thought. *Not bad at all, for a first try!*

The boy nodded his head in approval. 'Nice. I like it.'

'Okay, here we go...'

Trying to remember how he'd seen in done on TV, Steven drew the rod back over his head, the hook sailing back on the end of the line, and then he flicked it forward jerkily. The line shot out, the hook shooting over the pool, and it hit a rock on the far side and plopped back into the water.

*Well, okay. Still, it's my first go.*

Determined to get a good casting, he drew back the line and sent it out again. This time it was better; the hook dropped neatly into the centre of the pool. Steven settled himself more comfortably on the rock.

The sun had gone down a little more, the sky had become a little darker, and the breeze blew a little cooler, sending thin puffs of breath down the back of his neck. Yet Steven still found it pleasant, certainly much nicer than the girl's dream, with the old dark castle and bristling thorn-bushes, and the sudden drop through the air that had robbed him of all breath and sense.

The fish danced and glimmered under the water.

Steven tugged his earlobe. *I wonder...*

'Do you know what time it is?' he asked the boy.

The boy looked at him. 'Time? No.'

He turned back to concentrate on the fish.

*How long have I been here?*

With a slight tug of uncertainty, he realised he didn't know. There were no other clocks, the boy wore no watch, and certainly no other way of keeping time. There was only the clearing, the pool, the fish.

There was only the dream.

Abruptly, he felt a tug on the line.

*A fish!*

'Hey!' the boy cried. 'You got one!'

'Alright, here goes!'

Steven heaved back on the line with all his strength. The rod bent with the force of it and he gripped it tightly, the shaft scraping against his palms.

It arched further as the fish fought back, pulling the line deeper into the pool in its attempts to escape. Steven dug his feet in as, tail flapping wildly, the fish broke the surface.

'Get him!' the boy said. 'Grab him!'

Steven gave another heave and yanked the fish out of the water. Panting delightedly, he swung the rod in and the fish flopped into his lap.

'Ugh!'

It felt cold and slimy.

'Get him!' the boy exclaimed, bouncing up and down in excitement, his own rod forgotten. 'He'll get away!'

Laying his rod to one side, careful not to let the fish jump out of his lap, Steven gingerly took hold of it. Its scales slid wetly between his fingers. The hook protruded from its mouth beneath one round and panicked eye.

'It's okay,' he said. 'It's alright.'

Even though it was a dream-fish, not truly real, he still wanted to treat it with respect. It seemed the right thing to do, somehow.

With a skill he didn't know he possessed Steven brought one hand up and gripped the fish behind its head, holding it firmly so that it couldn't slide away. Then he took hold of the hook with the other and pulled it smoothly out of the fish's mouth, taking care not to snag its lip.

Then he took the fish in both hands and slipped it back into the pool.

The boy nodded approvingly. 'That's the way to do it!'

Steven pushed his hands underwater and washed them. 'Thanks.'

Now that he knew he could do a Summoning, he suddenly felt like leaving. He was done here, he knew.

Standing, he dusted himself off.

'I have to leave,' he told the boy. 'You can keep my rod.'

'Oh, are you sure?' the boy said. 'You can stay! You're a good fisherman!'

'I'd like to,' Steven said, 'but I have to go, sorry. Enjoy your fishing!'

He started to walk towards the edge of the clearing before realising he didn't know how to get out.

The girl's dream had ended when she woke up. That happened of her own accord and wasn't anything Steven had done - thankfully, he reminded himself – and so he had no idea of how to actually leave a dream once you'd entered it.

He thought about asking the boy, but something told him that he wouldn't know what he was talking about. He glanced back at the pool and saw the boy was leaning over the pool again, watching the fish.

Steven's rod was gone. It had vanished as if it had never existed in the first place.

Steven tugged his lower lip between thumb and forefinger.

*How to get out?*

Then he had an idea. He'd been able to Summon the fishing rod by wishing for it, so...

He stood still and closed his eyes.

*I wish to leave the dream*, he thought, clearly and strongly.

There was a slow hiss, like a balloon being let gently down, and then the clearing dissolved around him like water swirling down a drain.

And he was back with Orion.

He grinned. 'Did it!'

'How did it go?' the cat asked. 'Did you have success?'

Steven told him.

'Interesting,' the cat said. 'So you have learnt how to Summon, and how to leave a dream at a time of your choosing. Very good, Steven. Very good.'

'How long was I in there?' Steven wanted to know. He could have been in there for hours while Orion waited.

The cat shrugged a little. 'Not long. A matter of moments, perhaps.'

'Moments?' Steven gaped. 'But I was gone for – ages! It felt like a whole day!'

'Dream-time is different than the Dreamland itself,' Orion explained. 'What feels like a long time inside a dream is only a few minutes here. Do not fret.'

Orion believed the best way forward was to go into as many dreams as possible, and that way Steven would get used to Sleepwalking and Summoning.

'Good idea,' Steven said, as though he had a choice in the matter. He didn't think anything he said would change Orion's mind. Besides, there was a hot wriggle of excitement in his stomach, as he thought about what he could do next, where he would be...

'Something strange happened in the dream,' Steven said. 'I couldn't remember what it felt like back in the world. The real world, I mean. I remembered my name, and me, but...'

'Dreams drop that away,' Orion said over his shoulder. They had continued along the forest path, and there was only the peaceful sound of the wind passing through the trees. 'You're inside the dreamer's creation, so you don't have your own memories of waking with you. You still know how you are, though. It passes as soon as you step outside of the dream.'

*Oh*, Steven thought with a rush of relief, *that's alright then*.

Something else was on his mind – so many questions, all crowding in on each other like over-eager job applicants – and he said, 'How is it that some things are - ordinary, and real, and other things are made-up, out of someone's head, and yet you can see them right alongside each other here?'

'Everything is possible here,' Orion told him. 'Whatever someone dreams, can be made flesh. It just depends on the dreamer.'

'But the Minotaur, the huge man back at the fair, wasn't in a dream,' Steven said. 'He was walking about, doing stuff. There was a witch, too.'

'Well, over time, some dreams, or the figures from those dreams, become more powerful than others. If enough dreamers have the same dream for long enough, enough times, they gather power. It becomes bigger, stronger, more real. And eventually the figure steps outside the minds of dreamers and becomes something in itself, something you can touch, something living.'

Steven thought about it. Everyone knew what a witch or a mermaid was. He'd seen the Minotaur himself in storybooks. Someone must have dreamed them up, a long time ago, and told others...

And they dreamed of them too, bringing them to life night after night in the limitless space of their imagination. Over time, they must have grown and grown...

And now they were real in the Dreamland.

'That makes sense,' Steven said. 'So if lots of people dreamt about me, I'd become big and powerful? Is that how it works?'

Orion chuckled. 'No offence intended, Steven, but I'm not sure many people will be dreaming about you – ah!'

Ahead of them, peeping out of the undergrowth like a shy faun, was another dream.

This one was a bright burnished circle, bronzed and solid-looking.

Steven glanced at Orion.

'Go ahead,' the cat said. 'You longer need my permission. Just remember the rule, practice your Summoning, and you'll be fine. I'll be here waiting for you.'

Steven grinned, and went in.

It was a city.

A vast, sprawling, teeming city.

A city made entirely of glass.

Steven gazed about him in awe. He was standing before a multitude of triangles, each one as tall as a skyscraper. Through each clear wall Steven could see another triangle and then another, building after building advancing backwards as far as he could see.

Light spilled through the layers of glass, a liquid shimmer that was reflected back from all sides. It was akin to standing in a hall of mirrors.

All about the square were rows and rows of golden statues. They were arranged to look like people; one standing with legs spread firmly apart, arms crossed firmly over its chest as another by its side raised its hand imploringly. Next to them a tall statue bent over a smaller one as though checking something, clasping its tiny hand firmly.

He'd never seen anything like this before. Clearly it was the work of a master designer.

Looking around for the dreamer, he became aware of a slight humming, a vibration almost below the range of hearing. It was like hearing the hum of a beehive, except that instead of being potent and threatening it was contented and calm, the rhythm of a machine working just right, every component in perfect harmony with the other. Steven had the sense that the whole city was caught, poised on the brink of movement, and if he waited long enough, things would begin to move like a wound-up clock being released.

He had a clear image of the mechanism of his grandfather clock at home. How it needed seven turns to the right with the small silver key to wind it up. How his father made sure it was wound every week.

*Careful about things like that, my Dad. I wonder what he'd think about this place.*

*I bet he'd love it here.*

That was the first clear memory of home he'd had in a dream since arriving in the Dreamland. That was odd. Orion had just said he wouldn't remember anything. Why would he remember that? What made it different?

Was it something to do with the Clock? The Clock of Hours?

Then, in the corner of the square, he spotted what could only be the dreamer.

There was a small booth, the kind that sells newspapers and chewing gum on busy street-corners, and next to it stood a man, polishing a statue with a red cloth.

He had on something like an old-fashioned train conductor's uniform with trousers, shirt and a dark jacket. A work-belt brimming with tools was around his waist, and he wore a peaked cap on his head. Steven could see pens and what looked like a golden compass poking out of his top-pocket.

The dreamer was white-haired and looked to be fairly elderly, but he moved around sprightly, blowing on the statue's metal surface and then buffing it to his satisfaction.

As he moved to the next, nodding in pleasure, Steven came up to him. 'Hello!'

The dreamer turned around, greeted him with a smile of welcome.

'Hello there! How are you?'

'I'm fine,' Steven said. After meeting the boy in the pool he was more relaxed about talking to dreamers, since it didn't look like he'd wake them up just by speaking with them. 'How are you?'

'I'm good,' the man said. 'Do you like my city?'

'I do, very much,' Steven told him, and the man beamed with pride.

'I made this,' the man grinned. He looked like he could have been an engineer when awake, or perhaps an architect.

'It's beautiful here,' Steven said admiringly. 'Is everything made of glass?'

'All except these,' the man said, patting the statue he'd just been polishing. 'I wanted something big, grand, something that would make a statement. You can't normally make buildings out of glass, they wouldn't have withstood the elements much, but I always had ideas...'

Steven nodded politely. He was starting to realise that dreamers only wanted to talk about their dream and not much else.

He decided to try something. 'I wonder, did you see that thing on TV yesterday? The thing that everyone's talking about?'

The man stared at him blankly. He wore an unfocused, slightly glassy-eyed look, as if someone had just interrupted his train of thought and he was having trouble recapturing it.

For a moment, Steven wondered if he'd gone too far, but then the man said, 'These buildings are all set in a particular design, you know. If you have the time...'

It was as if he'd never asked in the first place.

'No, that's alright,' he said. 'I'll just have a look around, I think.'

'Good, you go ahead,' the man said. He produced a bottle of liquid from his tool-belt and began to spray the statue with it. 'It's all made of glass, you know!'

Steven walked off as the dreamer began to polish the statue vigorously with his red cloth. There were ways to talk to them without disturbing them; you just had to be careful, it seemed.

*Strange that no-one's told me their name so far, or anything actually about them.*

*Well, I don't suppose they think they need to. It is their dream, after all.*

He had just turned the corner when from behind there was a sharp crunch. An enormous crack raced through the glass triangle next to him.

He whirled. *What-?*

The dreamer was cowering on his knees in fear. His cap had fallen off and his bottle and cloth lay abandoned on the ground.

Bent over him, swathed in an iridescent robe, stood a figure that Steven recognised instantly.

His heart lurched in his chest.

*It's him!!*

It was the Dream Thief.

One hand clutched a thick black sack. The other was before the dreamer's face, fingers spread and rigid as though it sought to tear something from the air.

Even as Steven watched, wisps of colour began to seep outwards from the dreamer's mouth and eyes. Like a devilish magic trick, streams of power were being drained from his body. They gathered in a ball in the Dream Thief's hand.

Without warning, the square dipped to one side. There was another enormous *crack* and a jagged line raced through the ground, splitting the square open.

*It's falling apart!*

'Stop!' Steven shouted.

The Dream Thief glanced up, seeing Steven for the first time, and his cloak rippled like a mirage. He caught a glimpse of a sneer on the white face, deep in the depths of the hood.

'*Stop it!*' Steven shouted again. 'You're hurting him!'

The glass buildings were toppling, crumpling one by one like soggy paper. The statues were collapsing about him on all sides, shattering into shards as they hit the ground.

With a venomous hiss the Dream Thief ripped his hand away from the dreamer. He plunged the stolen light deep into the black sack, forcing it savagely down like a captured animal. Then his hand dived slipped into the gleaming robe.

The dreamer fell back, wheezing and gasping, hands clutching his throat.

The Dream Thief flung out his hand. Something like a wet clot of mud smashed into Steven's chest.

Everything went black.

*'Hoooo-ooooo...heeeee-eeeeee...'*

*Ouch...my head...*

Steven was lying prostrate on the ground, chest throbbing as though someone had struck him. Weariness flooded his body. He had no idea where he was, and the blood seemed to be swimming sickeningly round and round in his head.

*What happened - ?*

Steven lay very still for a moment, not moving, until the pounding in his head subsided a little and he felt better.

Then he remembered the dream; the city of glass, the dreamer with his cloth and bottle, cheerfully polishing his beloved statues. The Dream Thief intruding, bringing the dreamer to his knees. Sucking the dream-force from him like a leech draining blood.

Plunging it deep into the depths of the big black sack.

*What did he hit me with?* Steven rubbed his chest. There was a cold patch over his heart and he probed it carefully, trying to see if anything was broken.

He seemed to be alright. The only lingering effect of the Dream Thief's spell was a sense of cold around him, like he had wrapped Steven in an icy sack-cloth.

He hoped the dreamer was okay.

*That must have been what happened to me.*

As soon as Steven had seen the Dream Thief he'd gone rushing straight in. He'd dashed straight across, just like he had when he'd entered the first dream.

He could have gotten hurt.

Yet he couldn't help it. Seeing the bloated, swollen sack of the stolen dreams had infuriated him; he hated it on sight. His dream in there, along with all the others.

All of them stolen away by the Dream Thief.

*'Heeeee-heeeeee...haaaaa-laaaaa...'*

Slowly, he raised his head and looked blearily about.

He was lying in the middle of a strange group of plants.

There were enormous thistles, taller than he was; huge mushrooms with bulging grey flesh and purple seams running beneath their skin; sharp-looking nettles and other odd things he couldn't name.

Each plant was swaying gently back and forth as if brushed by an invisible wind.

*'Hoooooo-hoooooo...'*

Behind him, clustering tightly together as if clutching a secret, a clump of slender green plants rocked slowly to and fro. Long, reed-like branches sprouted from their tops that swept the air around them like feelers. As Steven glanced at them they bent towards him as if saying hello, and the tips of the branches touched his shoes.

*'Heeeee-teeeee...hooooo-haaaaaa...'*

In the middle of each plant was a cheery face, round and happy with a wide, chuckling mouth and two beaming eyes.

*'Hoooooo....'*

The plants were singing, a high, fluting melody that washed pleasantly against his ears. They sang the same words at the same time, moving together like fronds on the sea-bed stirred by an ocean current, and as they sang the other plants moved with them, drawn irresistibly by their song.

Steven smiled as he listened to it. It was soothing...

*It wasn't so bad here...* The Dream Thief's spell hadn't really hurt him, just thrown him out of the dream and sent him here.

*Why would he want to send me here, though?* The thought was fuzzy and ill-formed, and it drifted away without settling.

'Haaaaa-leeeee...hooooo-eeeee...'

Steven smiled again. It was a wide, dopey smile. The melody was louder now, blotting out everything else. He had the sudden urge to sit down, and saw that one of the mushrooms had a broad, seat-like cap that would be just right.

He put his chin in his hands and nodded along to the music.

The melody surrounded him, drew him in. Back and forth, back and forth...

'Hee-ee,' the plants sang. 'Hoo-aa...'

A swaying branch brushed his shoulder.

*Hmmm?*

He blinked suddenly. He'd closed his eyes for a moment.

The branch dropped away. Another one looped out and whispered across his foot.

*They're longer than I thought.* Steven yawned widely. He started to rock again on the mushroom.

*Wow, I'm tired. Really, really tired.*

'Hooo-hoooo,' the trees sang softly, seductively. 'Heeee-heeee....'

Steven yawned again. A great wave of exhaustion was rolling through him.

Funny – he didn't think he'd need to sleep in the Dreamland. That was how he went into dreams – other people were sleeping, and he didn't sleep, that wouldn't work for a Sleepwalker...

*I could sleep now, though...*

'Hooo-hoooo...'

That was a good idea. A great idea, actually. He deserved a nap after all he'd been through.  Fighting the Dream Thief, and getting a spell cast on you, and being thrown out of the dream miles away, and he didn't know exactly where he was anyway, did he? Nice of Orion to go off and abandon him, it wasn't fair, he deserved to sleep, he needed to sleep...

He felt a soft thump as he sat down on the ground. The mushroom was against his back, the cap pushing his head forward, and he knew that it would be better, was better, to lie down...lie on the loamy earth.

'Heeeeee....'

His eyelids felt heavy. Too heavy to hold up. He glimpsed the plants bending over him, eyes beaming cheerfully, mouths hooting in song.

*Sleep...*

He felt the soft caress of the branches as they gathered over him. They slid over his arms and crept up his legs. It felt good. He would sleep here for a while, and then get up and go on. The garden would be his bower, the grass his blanket...he would sleep here for a long time...a very, very long time...

'Ho there!' came a shout.

As if a firecracker had gone off by his ear, Steven jerked upright.

The weariness vanished from his mind. Fright took its place. He was lying prostrate on the ground, a net of branches covering him from head to toe.

A few moment longer, and he would have been lost.

'Hey-a!'

Steven sprang to his feet, tearing the branches from his clothes. They felt sticky, like the grasping tentacles of an octopus, and he flung them away.

The plants rocked away, looking mournful.

'Heeee.....'

*Now I know why he sent me here*, Steven thought. He wanted me to fall under their spell. The nearest plant sent another branch dancing towards him and he smacked it away with the palm of his hand.

'Hoooo....'

'Hey there!' came the voice.

A little man was skipping towards him through the plants. He was humming as he came, and every so often he would click his heels together in the air and chortle as though he'd just heard a tremendous joke.

He was clad in a bottle-green tunic and trousers and wore velvet sea-green boots on his feet. A huge floppy hat was crammed onto his head, the brim stitched and worn. His parchment-like skin was a rich nut-brown, and Steven instantly thought of a farmer's field with the earth freshly ploughed.

His eyes were round and twinkling.

'Ho!' he cried again. His voice was rich and round, resounding like the boom of a deep brass bell.

At the sound of it the plants became silent and flopped forward, branches drooping to the ground. They hung there together like chastised children. The rest of the plants in the garden followed suit, coming to rest as though weary of a game they had all been playing.

The little man ignored them completely, capering and dancing through the sagging fronds until he had come up to Steven.

'Hello there, Sleepwalker!' he said, sweeping the hat from his head in one smooth movement. He was completely bald, and his head gleamed like the smooth skin of an acorn. 'Very pleased to meet your acquaintance, so I am indeed!'

'Er, hello,' Steven said. 'How do you know I was a Sleepwalker?'

The little man laughed again. 'Why, what else could you be? A human boy, here? And certainly most folks know not to stray by the Singing Trees.'

'Oh, is that what they're called?' Steven, taking a step back from the hanging plants. They were limp and quiet now, but he was still wary of them after almost succumbing to their wiles.

'Indeed so,' the little man said. He jammed a long pipe of clay into his mouth. It started smoking instantly, sending alarming puffs of violet smoke past Steven's nose.

'The name's Merryweather,' he said. 'But you can call me Merry.'

'Hello,' Steven said. The little man seized his hand and pumped it firmly. For someone that size, he had a grip like a vice. Then he sat on a nearby toadstool.

Steven followed suit.

'Those things nearly made me fall asleep,' he said, pointing at the Singing Trees.

'Ah yes!' Merryweather took a long drag on his pipe and sent a puff of smoke towards them.   'Mischievous things, so they are!'

'Are they – dangerous?' Steven wanted to know.

'Dangerous? Goodness me, no!' Merryweather winked at him. 'Not a danger to you, are these boys. They're more...a hazard for the unwary, you catch my drift? They don't know what they're doing, so they don't.'

The nearest plant gave a small, sad *heeeeeee*, and a branch flopped onto Merryweather's shoulder as if to say, *sorry*. Merryweather brushed it gently off.

'Thanks for saving me,' Steven said earnestly. 'I don't know what I would've done if you hadn't come along. The Dream Thief sent me here, you see.'

At the mention of the name Merryweather turned his head and launched an alarming clot of sputum to one side. 'Paaaaah! *Him*! Cursed was the day he went over, I can tell you. No great loss, but still.'

'Over to...do you mean...?'

'Yes, to *him*.The keeper of nightmares.'

For the first time Merryweather looked solemn. Steven felt a trickle of fear at the thought of the black-garbed figure sitting atop of his throne of ebony. There was something about the way he kept his face hidden, and used the shadows like a mantle, that made him seem like a poisonous spider hanging at the centre of a web, waiting to catch the unwary.

The Dream Thief kept his face hidden too, Steven realised. What was it with disguising yourself if you were a bad guy? He felt a rush of anger and determination. If nothing else, he would unmask the Dream Thief, he thought. He would pull back the hood and see his face.

'So...the Dream Thief works for...the Lord?'

'Aye, that he does,' Merryweather said. 'A few such servants he has, those who choose to enter his service willingly, or those weak enough that he can bend to his purpose. Mighty clever he is, the Lord of Nightmares. There is some grand plan behind all of this, you mark my words, but I cannot glimpse it. Maybe you can grasp it, young Steven.'

'Maybe,' Steven said thoughtfully. 'Maybe.'

'Grand!' Merryweather exclaimed and, hopping off the toadstool, began jigging up and down. 'Look at the two of us, wasting away the day like a couple of old gossips! We need to be getting you back, so we do. A certain black-and-white feline will be wondering after you.'

So saying, he took the pipe out of his mouth and held it with the stem pointing downwards towards the earth. Then he began to circle it clockwise, round and round.

Around them the strange garden started to revolve. The plants spun, whirling round Steven, faster and faster with the revolutions of Merryweather's pipe. He felt dizzy.

'Hey-a!' Merryweather cried. 'Here we go!'

Steven couldn't see the garden at all, just streaks of light and darkness whipping past his head. He  held on tightly to the cap of the toadstool.

*Whoosh!*

There was a tug, like someone had just pulled at his collar, then the circle began to slow. As it settled, Steven saw they had left the garden behind and they were now back in the forest where he had first entered the dream of the glass city.

'There he is!' Merryweather said.

Some way away Orion was moving anxiously through the trees, casting over the ground as though trying to pick up a scent. Every few moments he would lift a paw up and say something, although they were too far away for Steven to make out what.

'Looks like we arrived just on time, Steven my boy!'

As the circle came to a complete stop Merryweather put his pipe back in his mouth and hopped out of the trees. Steven followed him, his legs feeling shaky.

Steven felt relieved to see Orion again and, unexpectedly, angry too. Hadn't he known the Dream Thief was near?

Orion's ears twitched as he heard them coming. Whirling round, rising on his hind legs, he bellowed something in a strange language and flung his paws out as though hurling a boulder at them.

For an instant Steven felt something rush towards him, vast and powerful, roaring like a steam-train, and then Merryweather held up his hand and said, *'Avert!'*

There was a sudden grinding sound, a buffet of air that blew Steven's hair back, and – nothing.

Orion gaped at them for a moment, then darted up. 'There you are!! I thought you were – you'd been – are you alright? Steven?'

'I'm fine,' Steven said, 'I'm okay. Merryweather saved me.'

'Then I must thank you, my friend,' Orion said gravelly, 'for I believed him lost.'

'Not lost as such,' Merryweather rejoined, chuckling. 'More...strayed from the path, I would say. Had a run-in with the Singing Trees, so he did.'

Orion frowned. 'How did you end up there?'

Quickly, Steven told him. He tried to stay calm when talking about how he'd encountered the Dream Thief, but it was difficult. By the end, he was visibly fuming, and Orion looked deeply crestfallen.

'Steven, I am sorry,' he said. 'I had no idea that he had grown so powerful so quickly. In all truthfulness, I did not expect to encounter him so soon, and you so ill-prepared. I ask you to forgive me.'

He bowed his head. Steven was taken aback; this was the first time he'd heard the cat apologise. It was also a little unsettling. He'd thought Orion knew what was going on.

As it turned out, Orion didn't seem to know much more than he did.

'Oh, it's not so bad,' Merryweather laughed. 'He's here now, am I right my boy?'

Feeling better, Steven grinned at him. 'Yeah. It's okay. I'm alright, really.'

Orion blew out a long breath. 'Good. That's good. Well, we must be on the move. These new developments trouble me, and I must speak with my Mistress. Merryweather, if you would be so kind?'

'Why, certainly!' Merry upended his pipe over the earth again and began to twirl it round. The forest began to move once more.

*Where are we going now?*

It seemed like they were never in one place for long; he was always moving to and fro, back and forth between dreams and the Dreamland. Steven suddenly longed to sit down, to set everything aside for a while and rest.

Yet he could only do that when the Dream Thief had been stopped, and whatever plan he was concocting had been foiled.

The forest spun around them in vivid slashes of emerald.

'Can you do this?' he whispered to Orion.

The cat looked a little shame-faced. 'No.'

Steven fought back an urge to laugh. 'Really? I thought - '

'I do have certain powers,' Orion said testily, 'but I haven't been granted this particular power. Not yet, anyway.'

The whirling circle slowed, and Steven could see they were in front of a long, white-bricked building with a wooden, triangular roof. It looked like a kind of church, or an abbey. 'What's this place?'

'This,' Orion told him, 'is the house of my Mistress.'

They came to a complete stop and Merryweather lifted up his pipe. 'There, my boy!'

'Thank you, old friend,' Orion said. 'Doubtless we will meet again soon!'

Steven felt a pang. 'You're leaving?'

'Indeed I must,' Merryweather said, tipping his hat to him. 'A-roving I must go, a–roving and a-roaming! But if you ever have need of me, call out my name, and I will be there. Remember, now!'

'I'll remember,' Steven said softly. 'And thank you.'

Merryweather winked at him and, with a hop and a skip, he was away again, boots thumping on the earth.

Sadly, Steven watched him go. 'I liked him. He was fun.'

After a moment, Orion said, 'This way.'

He went to a small door in the wall and tapped it three times.

As it opened, Orion said, 'Welcome to the House of Sleep.'

They came into a long, high room steeped in gentle light that crept in through high windows. It was filled with row upon row of pew-like beds, each with a figure lying under the sheets, slumbering deeply with their heads resting upon white pillows. Every so often one would move or stir, and a faint sigh would pass through the room.

Steven and Orion crept softly forward. The wooden floor was so exquisitely polished it gleamed like ivory, and their sounds of the passage made tiny little creaks in the quietness.

Steven tried to breathe as softly as he could. Just being here made him feel warm and at ease. A pleasant sensation of drowsiness came over him, as if he were at home in bed, descending into the slow depths of slumber.

Between the rows of beds, an avenue ran the length of the room. Orion began to make his way down. Steven made to follow before they were brought up short by a figure appearing suddenly before them, hands clasped.

It was an indistinct shape clad in a long flowing robe. Steven couldn't see it completely because it was nearly invisible.

It was as if someone had begun to sketch a woman in the air, making long lines that spoke of gentleness and warmth, the promise of rest after a long and wearying journey; and yet had set it aside half-way through the portrait, so that Steven saw an impression of before him, a sense of being brought into half-life.

No words were spoken aloud, but the figure inclined its head towards him, and he knew that he was welcome.

'The attendants of the House,' Orion whispered.

Now Steven could see more of them moving slowly between the beds, smoothing sheets down, tending the sleeping figures. He could only make them out by seeing the dust swirl in the wake of their passage; otherwise, they were utterly silent.

The figure in front of him made a motion.

'Come forward,' Orion said.

Steven stepped in front of the waiting attendant. As he came closer he could see a faint golden shimmer in the air, around where its heart would be. The figure motioned again, and he felt the pressure of what could have been a hand on his head.

A long, luxurious feeling steeped through him. He breathed in, a huge, swelling breath, and said, *'Ah!'*

It was as if he had slept for a week, a deep, undisturbed, healing slumber, and had awakened feeling completely refreshed, reborn anew.

The figure lowered its hand and moved away.

Steven met Orion's electric gaze.

He could feel tears brimming in his eyes, but he didn't want to cry.

Orion nodded.

'The gift of my Mistress,' he said.

After a moment, they went on between the beds. Steven glanced down at the figures on either side, but he could make out nothing of their features. A layer of wispy gauze seemed to lie over them, so that he saw their peace and rest through a veil.

At the end of the room, Orion stopped. 'Can you wait here, Steven? I must speak with my Mistress. We will decide on what best to do now.'

Steven nodded agreement. There was an empty bed nearby and he sat down on the edge. An attendant brushed by, and Steven could feel a raised chin, uplifted eyebrows, an question asked without speaking: *sleep?*

Steven shook his head gratefully. *No.*

The attendant went past, a brief flicker of gold in the air.

He watched Orion approach the wall. A narrow bar of shadow lay underneath the nearest window, and as Orion crept into it he gave a brief shake of his head as though trying to clear his ears.

There was a slight, silvery chime, as though a bell had been struck, and Orion vanished. Steven laughed softly. He had ceased to be surprised.

There were rustles, murmurs; someone turned over on a nearby bed. Steven waited.

His thoughts drifted like the motes of dust in the falling beams of light.

The Dream Thief. Somehow, it seemed wrong, to be thinking of him here, and yet his thoughts kept coming back to him, that white-faced emissary of the Lord of Nightmares, clad in his shimmering robe.

*What was his plan?*

What did they want to do?

Stealing dreams...why? Orion had said something before that Steven couldn't quite remember. Something to do with dreaming yourself bigger...

*If you had a lot of dreams, you would have an awful lot of power*, he mused. What could you do with that?

What would one of the Three do with that?

He strained to think, there in that lighted room with the peaceful sleepers all around. His green eyes clouded over, like the reflection of storm clouds passing over the ocean.

He couldn't get to it. Maybe Orion would know, after speaking to the Mistress.

*I wonder how long they'll be.*

Idly, he picked at a nail. The Dream Thief's hooded face lingered in his mind. He could almost make it out, somehow...there was something...

*A clown's face.*

He frowned. Why did he think that? Something to do with a clown?

*I-*

A little way down the room, deep within the shadows, someone was watching him. Steven bolted upright, blinking widely like he had just been startled awake. A man in a mottled green and grey robe was standing there, looking at him.

*I've seen him before!*

It was the man from the fair!

Steven pointed. 'Hey - '

His voice was loud in the silence and several of the attendants paused in their duties and looked over at him. He could feel their disapproval.

'Sorry,' he whispered, 'it's - '

The man had vanished.

No-one was there. The shadows were empty. He had completely disappeared.

*Aaah!!* Steven ground his teeth in frustration. Who was he? What did he want?

Several of the attendants looked over at where he had been pointed, then at each other. He could sense their shrugs as they dismissed it.

'I'm not mad,' Steven murmured to himself. 'There was someone there.'

*Tap.*

What?

*Tap, tap.*

He glanced around.

*Tap, tap.*

It was a small noise, almost imperceptible, but it worried at him like a loose tooth.

*Where's it coming from?*

The attendants were continuing to move about the room. They hadn't heard it.

Steven approached the wall. It was made from smooth white brick, and looked unmarked – although now he looked closely there was a faint outline, as though it had been made many years ago and then Time had smoothed it over.

He traced the line with a finger.

A door.

Furtively, he glanced around. The attendants were drifting between the beds.

He pressed his hand against the wall.

It opened outwards in the shape of the door.

Beyond, there was a small patch of grass.

Steven darted quickly through.

He found himself in a small walled garden. Over the high white walls he could see trees and hear the throaty warble of bird-song. Ivy clung to the bricks, and there was a wooden bench to one side.

He did not see the door swung shut behind him, blending seamlessly into the wall again.

The grass was growing wild, speckled with daisies. At the edge were crimson roses, pale tulips, violets and lilies, glowing sunflowers bending to catch the sun, dandelions with their crowned heads of seeds ready for the next puff of wind.

Steven stared at the centre of the garden. A raised block of stone waited there.

A small well capped it. It was built from drab grey brick, and weeds were encroaching on the cracked slabs beneath. There was nothing to distinguish it as being out of the ordinary.

Yet his eye was drawn to it irresistibly. As the magpie spies the glittering light in the leaves, so did Steven fix upon the well. He knew, at once, that he must look within.

*It* was there. What *it* was, he didn't know, nor did he possess the words to say; he only knew he must go to it.

Slowly, deliberately, Steven stepped onto the block of stone. He knelt before the well, placed his palms on the edge, and looked down.

Beneath the lip of the well, lapping gently at the walls as though stirred by a current far below, Steven saw water. It was as black as pitch. He could see no light in the depths and yet somehow the water shone, gleaming darkly like liquid onyx.

His eyes widened as he peered down into it. The well seemed bottomless, a tunnel excavated deep into the earth. Steven felt he could topple forward, plunge down into the water and enter a passageway that would take him to...

As he watched, the water gleamed brighter, a dark illumination that met and held fast in his eyes. The rippling of the dark bright water pulled at him, urged him to throw himself into the well.

Yes! He would fling himself headfirst into the water! He was doing so even now, slipping beneath the black surface, feeling it enclose him, welcome him even as he knew that he still knelt before the well, hands on the rim. He was both outside it and within it.

Slowly, the bottom of the well rose up to meet him. It was silty and wet, long undisturbed by the passage of human feet, and as he descended a hole opened before him, a road of welcome that stretched away like an unbroken ribbon.

At the tunnel's end, winking faintly in the distance, Steven saw a point of bright light, glittering like a star in the night sky. He knew he must reach it – he must get there!

As if sensing his urgency, the star began to move towards him. Slowly at first but then faster and faster, growing as it came, swelling and shining, a perfect circle of white light that became a woman's face, hanging before him in the dark tunnel.

She was perhaps in her middle years, and her auburn hair was cropped short around her sleeping face. For sleeping she was: lying in bed, her head on a pillow, a blanket pulled up to her chin. Her face lay to one side, half-shadowed.

He floated in the void.

*Who was she?*

Her image burst apart. A dazzling burst of light struck him. Steven jerked backwards, arms out-flung against the piercing light, and then he was kneeling on the stone once more as the dream rose up towards him.

It came slowly, ascending up through the dark well water like a long-buried treasure being brought towards the light of day.

*That's her dream*, he thought, and a bright sense of wonder and fear broke in him.

The dream reached the surface, hesitated, and like a child placing a toe in the unfamiliar water of the ocean, it slipped gently through and into the Dreamland.

Riding the breeze like a hovering bird, it rose up before Steven's face. He couldn't tear his eyes away from it. It came up, over his head, passed over him.

This was the Well of Dreams; the link between the waking world and the Dreamland. Now Steven understood how dreams were made manifest here, how they made their passage after being nourished in the minds of their dreamers. They were made, thought out, crafted out of raw creation in his world, the world of wakefulness; then they made the voyage through the Well to come into full being here, in the Dreamland. The Well of Dreams was the passageway, the conduit, the doorway.

There was a light caress over his hair. Somewhere, in the kingdom she had brought to life, the dreamer walked.

Steven turned to follow it.

The Dream Thief was standing behind him.

His robe shimmered and rippled like a lizard preening its scales. The black sack was in his hand, fingers curled around it like a vice. His lip was curled in a cold sneer.

'H - ' Steven got out -

'*Silence!*' the Dream Thief snarled. He made a clutching gesture before Steven's throat.

Instantly, Steven's voice was choked off. He fell back against the Well, the stone scraping his back. Coughing and gagging, he strove desperately to cry out.

It was no use. He had been rendered mute.

The Dream Thief seized hold of the hovering dream. Eyes blazing in triumph, he squeezed it between his fingers.

'You lose, Steven,' he grinned, then thrust the dream into the big black sack.

'*No*,' Steven managed to get out, wheezing for air. '*You can't.*'

'Oh, you can speak,' the Dream Thief said. 'Quite the little fighter, aren't you? Well, let's see how much fight you have in you.'

He extended one pointed fingernail in front of Steven's chest. Then, in a vicious corkscrewing motion, he twisted it round.

*Aaah!!*

Steven would have screamed if he had been able. A hot stabbing sensation burst over his heart as though a hot blade had been plunged into it. The garden around them spun in chaotic disarray. The walls became a blur. The bright flowers whirled away into nothing.

In its place appeared a gloomy woodland path. Dead leaves drenched the ground, speckled with dirt and spotted with lichen. The thick, gnarled trees were intertwined like the bodies of serpents, and their gnarled branches hid the light away. A thin mist shrouded them.

Steven fell away from the Dream Thief, rubbing his throat. He saw that they were totally alone on the path; the House of Sleep had vanished. Odd echoes rang in his ears, as though someone nearby was shouting for help.

*What can I do!?*

This was no dream; he could summon no weapon, bring nothing to bear here.

The Dream Thief drew himself up, eyes gleaming imperiously in the shadows of the hood.

'*Run*,' he hissed.

Steven ran.

He fled in a bright steam of fright through the dark wood. The mist hid the path before him; the mounds of decaying leaves stuck to his feet like malicious fingers; unseen branches whipped him in the face.

Behind him the Dream Thief came, running easily over the ground, snickering softly in the chase. The black sack whispered against his robe.

*Must get away!*

Steven put on a fresh burst of speed, lifting his feet high above the carpet of leaves, striving to gain ground.

It was like moving through glue. The leaves seemed to grip tighter. The mist seemed to grow thicker. The trees seemed to loom out of clots of shadow, aged trunks crooked and sly, leering at him like old, mean faces.

Then an invisible branch tripped him and he fell, tumbling to the ground. Cold, wet leaves engulfed his face.

Behind him, he heard the Dream Thief come to a halt.

He had never felt so exposed in all his life. He was completely at the mercy of his enemy. He expected a hand to grasp the back of his neck, or a foot to come stamping down on his back.

None of those things happened.

*What's he waiting for?*

Slowly, Steven pushed himself up on his arms.

Then he froze.

Waddling across the path before him was an enormous spider. Black and furry, eight spindly legs working with a horrible purpose, it scuttled away into the shadows.

Steven let his breath out slowly. Although he wasn't terrified of spiders like his Mum, he wasn't terribly fond of them either. What he was really frightened of was –

Beneath a nearby tree, coiling in the shadows, something hissed. Steven knew what it was even before he turned his head to see it.

A snake.

What he was really frightened of were snakes.

The blunt, spear-shaped head came forward and the bared fangs gleamed. The forked tongue flickered.

Above him, high in the crooked branches, a leathery shape croaked. The vulture's beak was old and yellowing, its head bare of feathers. The shadow of its wings hung over Steven.

Watching the snake, every part of him taut with fear, Steven got up as slowly as he dared.

*If I don't move fast – if I don't startle it – it won't –*

Then he saw who stood on the path before him, and all thoughts of the snake fled his mind.

It was a cowled figure, swathed in black, darker than the darkness itself. Steven had last seen him in the throne-room, on his seat of ebony.

It was the Lord of Nightmares.

*We meet again, boy*, he said.

Steven shivered at the sound of his voice. It was the sound of ice breaking, the clicking of a scorpion inside a favourite shoe, a door swinging open in a haunted house in the dead of night. It was a hundred dreadful things given mouth and lips and the will to speak.

He swallowed thickly. 'I'm not afraid of you.'

The shrouded head tilted. *Then you are very stupid, boy.*

Steven could feel the coldness of his gaze, the utter disregard, as though he were simply an annoying insect who had blundered into his path and could be crushed in an instant.

He glanced over his shoulder. The Dream Thief stood patiently nearby, waiting. Like a dog eager for his master's command.

*You don't belong here,* the shadow said. *You know that, don't you? So foolish. You come looking for the one who takes dreams. Now you have found him. My servant. He does my work.*

Standing before the black-shrouded figure, Steven felt terribly frightened. It was a pure and icy fear that reached into the hollows of his bones, the chambers of his heart. It took all his strength to say, 'You can't do that. It's wrong.'

*I do precisely as I please*, said the Lord of Nightmares. *And I shall do as I please with you.*

He lifted up his hands, the pale, thin fingers stealing out from the ends of his robe like blind worms bred underground, and he flung them outstretched at Steven –

- and something rose up before him, a thick cloud of shadow that began to simmer and writhe, a mustering darkness that drew together in an unimaginable shape –

- and light burst from behind Steven.

Silver. Gold. Burning, blazing.

Setting the very air afire.

Flaming out in unison, they banished the shadows, sent the pillar of darkness tumbling skittering away. The mist shredded like an old rag. The trees, stripped of their cloaks of concealment, suddenly seemed old, weary, clinging together lest they topple helpless to the ground.

The twin fires grew. They flamed brighter, hotter; as it was though Steven stood in front of a vast torch, a signal flare that cast back the night, drove back fear, tiredness, pain. He felt it erupt inside of him.

Caught in the gleaming radiance the Lord of Nightmares shrank away in dismay. *You dare to interfere!!*

Cool, silvery tones rang out. *We do nothing. It is champion against champion, as it is ordained. We keep the Balance.*

*And to keep the Balance only.* Warm, rich words. *Consider this a warning.*

The shadow shrank further into itself, shrivelling like a burning cobweb.

*Very well. I shall not raise my hand to him. But I promise you, boy – the time will come when you call me Lord.*

Then the cowled figure was gone.

Steven gasped. He felt as if an icy hand, gripping his heart with a remorseless strength, had slackened and fallen away. He was free again.

The twin fires began to dim.

Steven held out his arms imploring. 'No! Don't go!'

*We must*, said the Maiden. There was a faint shimmer on the air, a garland of silver. *We can have no part in this.*

*It is between the two of you alone*, said the Earl. Gold flickered like the dying embers on a hearth. *Fare you well!*

Then they, too, were gone.

And cringing on the path, cowering like a whipped animal, was the Dream Thief.

Steven swelled with power. It roared in him like a tidal wave; he was so full of strength he felt he must burst. 'You!'

The Dream Thief ran.

Steven went after him. He ran as fast as he could, drawing every on every ounce of force the Maiden and Earl had bestowed upon him.

Yet the Dream Thief was quick, as though he understood his destruction was upon him. He kept just in front of Steven, bobbing and darting just out of reach. His robe streamed behind him like a tattered sail.

Steven put on a fresh burst of speed.

*Come on!!*

The black sack swayed mockingly.

*Almost there!*

He felt the power being to ebb away. He couldn't keep this up much longer.

With the last of his strength he sprang forward and threw himself at the Dream Thief.

His fingers snagged the edge of his robe.

*Got him!!*

The Dream Thief shrieked like a jackal and tumbled. Steven landed painfully on his elbows, his fingers entangled.

'Got you,' he panted. 'Got you now.'

The Dream Thief thrashed wildly about, seeking to escape. The robe was hot in Steven's hands as though it burned. A playing card flicked against his face and he shook his head, sending it to one side.

*What - ?*

The Dream Thief threw the sack away. It thumped against the base of a tree and Steven heard a multitude of plaintive cries as the dreams within were shaken crudely about.

'Let's see who you really are!' he shouted, grappling for the hood –

- and the Dream Thief pulled something wet and gleaming out of his robe. He drove it straight into Steven's face.

'*Agh!*' It was fiercely cold, and seeped into his mouth and nose like oil.

*I can't breathe!*

He choked, trying to pull away.

Blackness swarmed around his eyes. Dimly, at the edge of his vision, he could see the Dream Thief getting to his feet.

He giggled. 'Told you you shouldn't have meddled, Sleepwalker. Let's see how you like *this* dream!'

Then, just as Steven was swallowed up, he seized hold of the Dream Thief's ankle.

There was a wail, and the dream sucked them down.

It was like swimming through a storm-tossed ocean. Steven couldn't see, he couldn't hear, he couldn't feel. He was in the middle of a clinging knot of darkness that rang away on all sides. It was chill and empty. Somewhere nearby he could sense the Dream Thief moaning and keening.

Then, abruptly, his vision cleared.

He was standing in a street, looking up at a house. An ordinary house, much like his own in the waking world. The walls were flat and grey, the windows empty. A gravel path lead to the front door.   A circular window in the peaked roof told him there was an attic.

There was no sign of the Dream Thief.

There was no wind, no stars. The night sky was as black and thin as crepe. Dim orbs of streetlamps hung like bloated eggs.

Steven walked backwards as fast as he could.

It did no good. He bumped against an invisible barrier before he had got three feet.

*Try something else.*

He thought, very strongly and clearly, *I wish to leave the dream.*

Nothing happened. He stayed exactly where he was.

*I wish to leave the dream*, he thought again.

Same result.

He looked up at the house, chewing his lip.

*I guess I'm stuck here.*

Then, high in the attic window, the Dream Thief appeared. His hood was down and his white, mask-like face floated in the gloom. It was strangely blurred, as though Steven saw him through smoke. It was clear, though, that the Dream Thief was smirking.

And suddenly, with a hot gush of rage within him, he was sick of it: the running, the chasing, the sense that he was blundering around in the dark searching for answers, always waiting for someone else to flick on the light.

'Right,' he muttered, and marched up to the front door.

He pushed it open.

The door collapsed away from its hinges. There was a bang as it hit the floor which seemed to echo shake the whole house.

The hallway was empty. Shadows spilled over the ruptured floorboards.

Steven stepped carefully over the broken door, listening for any sounds above his head.

The living room was on his right. A brown sofa and ragged armchair had been completely slashed to pieces as though a wild animal had attacked them in a fit of rage. A few rusty springs poked up askew from within the shattered remnants. Wafts of cotton covered the patchy carpet like bizarre confetti.

At the end of the room a stump of splintered wood was sticking out of a huge TV. A crumpled coffee-table was over on one side before a pair of shattered French windows. Outside, Steven could make out a small garden, overgrown and choked with weeds. Someone had thrown a lawnmower into the pond.

*Who on earth - ?*

*I don't think I want to meet whoever dreamed this up.*

The very air seemed frigid, as though all warmth and light had been drained away.

Yet didn't he, from time to time, have bad dreams? Dreams where strange, unpleasant things happened? And didn't he go along with it, carried by the dream's unspooling flow like an unwilling passenger on a rollercoaster, unable to get off but at the same time expecting the next corner, the next sharp jerk and twist? And the next? And the next?

*I can't go anywhere, anyway. Not while* he's *upstairs.*

*And I can get things, here. Stuff that can help me.*

The next door led to the kitchen. This was even worse. It looked like a bomb had gone off inside it.

The dining table was broken completely in half, the tiled floor shattered into fragments. Glass and chips of stone crunched under his feet. The cupboard doors hung drunkenly from their hinges.

No sound from above.

Steven went to the foot of the stairs and peered up into the darkness.

He tried the light switch.

Broken.

He put a foot on the first stair, expecting a creak.

Silence.

*I'm not going up there without a light.*

*Wait a second –*

He concentrated, focusing hard. *I need light -*

His palm thrummed. Power gathered in his arm. He remembered his Dad's shed, weathered and brown. He sometimes went in there in the summer, when his Dad worked on the garden. There was a lawnmower inside, trowels, spades and forks. Fuses in a tin on a shelf. Next to that –

*Thick, heavy, black surface, a loop of cotton on the end –*

And there it was, sitting chunkily in his hand.

*A torch.*

Steven clicked it on. A fat beam of light speared through the darkness.

Slowly, he went up.

A small landing at the top. A bedroom to one side, a bathroom on the right.

The attic above, white panel flat and closed.

Again, no sound.

*How can I –*

Something rustled in the bedroom.

Spinning round, Steven sent the torchlight flicking through the doorway. It lit the edge of a bed, a slashed mattress, torn sheets.

*What was that?*

The shifting came again. It sounded like something was alive in there.

*A rat?*

Heart thudding, he crept in.

The bedroom, too, had been torn apart. A dressing-table had been rent to pieces and flung against the farthest wall. The carpet had been peeled back, exposing the bare boards, and a large wardrobe by the window tilted wearily to one side. The curtains hung in shreds.

There was nothing there.

Steven started to back out, then  –

*I haven't looked under the bed.*

The torch-beam crept to the edge of the ruined mattress.

It was straight out of every horror film he'd ever seen. Taking a deep breath, he grabbed the corner of the mattress and yanked it up. The torch-beam stabbed into the space below.

Nothing there either. No ghoul, no bogeyman, no vampire waiting to spring.

He swept the torch back and forth, checking each corner. There was only dust, and a few mothballs.

*Whew.*

Then the doors of the wardrobe creaked open, and the jacket rose up in the air.

It was empty. No-one was wearing it.

It was a large black suit jacket, the kind his Dad sometimes wore when he went out to a posh dinner. It looked like there was someone inside, otherwise how did it move, hang there in the air like that?

But there wasn't anyone.

' -what- ' Steven said.

Rippling, billowing, the jacket came at him.

Steven fell back. Out of the bedroom. Into the hall. Jerking stiffly, it followed. It looked like a marionette with the strings cut.

'No - ' Steven said. 'Get away - '

The jacket came on. The sleeves lifted up. No arms, no fingers wriggling at the end. Just empty space. Somehow, that was worse.

A cold, high giggle floated down from the attic.

Steven waved the torch in front of him, sending the light darting over the pin-striped lapels, the neat pockets.

'Get away from me!' he cried.

The jacket glided forward and the sleeves pressed at his face and neck. They rubbed against him, smooth as worm-skin. They crept across his face, pressed against his nose. He felt a button against his cheek.

*Think! Come on!*

What was there in a house? What could he use?

*A TV – fridge – cups – magazines -*

The sleeves smoothed over his cheeks, his lips.

*Carpet – fish – no –*

They were trying to get inside his mouth.

Then he remembered, with a cool clarity, his Mum's sewing basket. Brown and orange and round as pumpkin, it had sat in the corner of the living room for as long as he could remember. On weekend afternoons his mother would take it out and do her sewing, fingers working deftly on shirts or shorts or whatever needed doing, humming to herself, her gaze far away as the needle dipped and darned.

*Inside there were needles – cotton – thread – and -*

A burst of pressure in his hand.

*- scissors.*

He was holding scissors. Large, gleaming, weighty.

Sharp.

Blades open.

Steven brought them up - under the arm of the jacket - *snip!*

He tore a hole right over the heart.

The jacket paused. It hung still, as though confused by what had happened.

*Snip!* Steven stuck the scissors forward again, ripping the collar.

The jacket shrank away. Steven followed.

It drifted back into the bedroom, arms tucked by its sides. Steven had the scissors out in front,   jabbing at it. *Snip! Snip!*

'Come on,' he snarled. He advanced like a demented tailor.

The jacket flew back to the wardrobe. Steven laughed. The scissors felt weighty and strong in his hand. He snapped them shut. *Snip!*

'What are you going to do now?' he cried. 'Huh?'

Then the wardrobe shuddered like a dying animal, and more clothes oozed out.

There were jackets and shirts and trousers and shorts. Blue and white and green and yellow, puffed and swollen as though they had been underwater for a long time. There was even a pair of socks, he saw incredulously, bobbing menacingly before him like a pair of boxing gloves.

'Oh,' he said, quietly.

They came at him in a rush. Their silence was awful.

He fought them. Plunging the scissors in and out, snapping the blades shut on sleeves and collars and legs, he kicked and pulled.

It was no good. They pressed around him, choking, clutching, drowning.

A sleeve slapped across his mouth, shutting off his cries. Another covered his eye.

Steven twisted away, trying to wrench his arms free.

A shirt clamped on his hand, covering the scissors. He couldn't move his fingers.

There was a crash as the attic door was flung open and the Dream Thief leapt out and down the stairs. Another high giggle lingered on the air. Then he was gone.

Steven couldn't breathe. Panic rattled his heart and lungs, drummed meaty fists inside his head. A sock was worming its way into his ear.

Something -

*What?*

He strained, trying to reach it.

*- a flash of green -*

A pair of trousers tackled him, knocking him down.

*- Ho! -*

61

And Steven knew.

He struggled in desperation, tearing at the clothes covering his face. The scissors were lost – he forget them, pulling at the fabric covering his mouth. His eyes, nose, head was covered.

He had to get his mouth free. Had to.

A shirt clung to his torso, squeezing like a python.

He dug his fingernails in, wrenched it away. Took a huge breath.

'*Merryweather!*' he bellowed. '*Merryweather!*'

*'Hey-a!'*

The disembodied clothes froze. Steven gasped; it was like being encased in a frozen straitjacket.

Then slowly, like a deflating cushion, they collapsed in a heap.

*'Hoy! Ho!'*

He sprang to his feet, tearing the empty clothes away. Kicking limp shirts and trousers into a corner, he checked himself frantically all over, making sure nothing was left.

*'Hey there!'*

Warm light, rich as honey, spilled into the room. It lifted Steven's spirits, gladdened his heart.

The walls of the house seemed to hollow out, to become as thin as tissue.

*'Hey!'*

Steven could hear Merryweather hopping and jigging beneath the window.

'I'm here!' Steven cried, rushing out onto the landing –

- and the floor sagged underneath him.

'Huh?' He glanced down.

*What's happening?*

His feet were sinking slowly into the carpet. It rose about his legs like quicksand.

*What now??*

Quickly, he tried to lift his feet up, but it was no use. The floor had taken a firm grip on him, and even as he watched he sank further and further down.

'Merryweather!' he called. 'Help!'

The nearby wall exploded in a cloud of powder. One moment it was standing upright, the next an enormous hole erupted through it and Steven was coughing and spluttering in the debris.

*Crack – crack – crack –* the stairs fell like a row of dominoes.

'Ho there! Young master!'

'I'm in here!' Steven shouted.

Now the floor was up to his waist. It felt cold and muddy, like clay. His legs were going numb.

Then the house split apart.

It went to pieces as swiftly as if a hurricane had roared down from the sky and smashed it to kindling. The remaining walls folded and splintered; the roof bulged in the centre and then split open; the floor, gripping him tightly one moment, dissolved into a murky puddle and drained away the next.

Steven was free. He was left standing on a patch of empty ground, inside the faint outline of what had once been the house. Merryweather was beaming cheerfully at him.

'Steven, my boy!' he cried. 'Wasn't too long ago we were saying farewell, was it now? Lucky I happened to be stopping by, hey-a?'

Steven brushed flakes of paint from his hair. 'I'm certainly glad to see you. Thanks for coming. Again!'

'Ah, now,' Merryweather winked, 'that was the deal, was it not? Say my name, and I'll come a-calling. Mind you, that's once!'

He held up two stubby fingers in front of Steven's eyes. 'Only two left now, have you. More than that, and I can't help you. So choose carefully, if you would be calling on my aid again.'

Steven didn't like to think about what kind of situation he'd be in if he needed help like that again.

'What were you doing wandering in a dream like this, anyhow?' Merryweather went on. 'A body could come to harm here, so they could.'

'Well, it wasn't exactly my idea,' Steven said ruefully, and told him what had happened at the House of Sleep. He described meeting the Lord of Nightmares in the wood, the mad scramble with the Dream Thief, and then finding himself here and having to fight the empty clothes.

'The Dream Thief got away again,' he finished. 'He's beaten me every time, so far.'

'Never fear, young master!' Merryweather exclaimed. 'Twice now you have faced him in dreams, yes? And twice now he has given you the slip. The third time is the charm, mark my words, oh yes indeed!'

'If you say so,' Steven said. 'I've had just about all I can manage of dreams for a while, I think.'

Merryweather eyed him speculatively for a moment.

Steven looked awful; he was covered in chips of wood and flakes of paint and his face was drawn and white. There were deep shadows under his eyes. He looked, you might say, like someone who hadn't slept in a long, long time.

'Ah, you've been through the mill, right enough,' Merryweather said at length. 'Come, I know just the place for you. Rest and a good meal is what you need.'

He whipped his pipe out and began to spin it over the ground. The empty ground about them began to revolve dizzyingly.

'One thing before we arrive, mind,' Merryweather said, 'You weren't hurt now, were you? Not cut or scratched, in that nasty little place?'

'Cut?' Steven said. He ran a hand over his arms and legs, seeing if he had been hurt. There was nothing; he'd escaped unscathed. 'No, I'm fine.'

'Good,' Merryweather said, eyebrows twitching like two large caterpillars. 'Terrible bad luck if you were, now. Very bad to let anything get a piece of you here, if they wish you ill. A drop of your blood, a hair – even a scrap from your clothing would do the trick, sometimes. Be careful of that, Steven.'

*Good job I didn't cut myself with my own scissors*, Steven thought.

The twisting vortex reached a peak and began to slow. They had arrived in a wide green meadow. Nearby was a small cottage with a thatched roof and rounded wooden door. A chimney sent up small puffs of smoke.

'Is this it?' Steven asked. 'Are we here?'

'Aye, this is the place,' Merryweather said, they came to a stop. 'This here's an old friend of mine, now.'

Tucking his pipe away, he went to the cottage door and rapped smartly upon it.

'Coming!' called a cheerful voice from within.

Steven glimpsed a circular pattern on the door that stirred something in his memory. It was a perfect circle with twelve spokes radiating outwards at equal intervals. A strange mark was in the centre.

*That looks like a –*

Then the door opened and an old woman stood there smiling.

She had light grey hair drawn back into a neat bun, and her eyes were bright and dancing. She wore a flour-covered apron over an old pinafore and comfy-looking slippers on her feet.

'Well, if it isn't visitors,' she said in a tone of delight. 'Merryweather, you old rascal! It's been too long, my dear!'

Wiping her hands on a dishcloth, she tucked it into her apron and scooped the little man up to give him a bone-shaking hug. Steven looked on in askance. He wasn't sure he could survive an embrace like that right now; he felt like he might fall to pieces at any moment.

Plonking Merryweather back on the ground, she looked Steven up and down. 'Well now! And who you might you be?'

'This is Steven,' Merryweather said, who was having trouble straightening his clothes. 'He's a Sleepwalker.'

'Of course you are!' the woman exclaimed. 'I've heard all about you. Well, come in, come in!'

She motioned him inside. Steven looked at Merryweather quickly.

'Oh, it's fine,' Merryweather laughed. 'We're old friends. Don't worry.'

'You poor boy,' the woman said, smiling at him sympathetically. 'You look all shaken up. There's no trouble here, I can promise you. Only a hot drink and something good to eat, if you do fancy it.'

'Okay,' Steven sighed. It was a nice offer, and the old woman looked very friendly, but he didn't have it in him to be polite right now. The shaky feeling inside him had increased and he knew he'd have to sit down or he would collapse on the spot.

Abruptly, he had a sudden, jolting image of waking up in his own bed, the world around him frozen and still; and what had happened since then tumbled through his head like a pair of madly spinning dice.

*How long ago was that?* He asked himself. It could have been a year ago.

He was tired; so very tired.

The woman beckoned him inside the cottage.

'I must be going, my boy,' Merryweather said, giving him a wave. 'Until we meet again!' Steven didn't have the will to protest. 'Bye, Merry. Thanks again!'

The little man tipped his hat to him, winked, and then bounded away, whistling a tune.

'Wait!' Steven called after him. 'What about Orion - '

But he was already gone.

'Never you fret, now,' the woman said, giving him a friendly pat on the back. 'Right this way.'

She led him into a large, bright kitchen. A pot of stew bubbled on the stove and the oven was humming away with the scent of fresh bread in the air. There was a vase of fresh flowers on the table. Through the window Steven saw a small yard, where chickens with feathers as yellow as gold bobbed and pecked at the earth.

'You sit yourself down,' the woman said, guiding him to a chair, 'and I'll bring you something. A growing boy like you, you need feeding up!'

Steven smiled at her, but he couldn't speak.

He slumped down in the chair and put his head in his hands.

Steven held his eyes closed. Somewhere, as if in the far distance, he could hear the woman bustling about the kitchen, clucking and whistling to herself. There came the sound of water running, the kettle boiling.

He wanted to push it all away; to run and hide somewhere far, far from here. It was too much.

He felt a hot warmth on his hands; realised he was crying. He missed his Mum and Dad. He wanted to go home.

'Here, now,' the warm voice came, over the whistling of the kettle. 'Have a cup of tea.'

He felt a hot mug being placed into his hands. He couldn't look up, ashamed of his tears, but he managed, 'T-thank you.'

A hand, surprisingly firm, squeezed his shoulder.

Steven held the steaming mug under his nose. The tea smelled rich and strong, with hints of cinnamon and nutmeg, and the scent seemed to flow into his mouth and throat, unwinding down into his stomach, leaving warmth and calm in its wake.

He took a tentative sip and the hot liquid rolled over his tongue.

There came a clanking and clattering of plates, and then the kind woman was handing him a tray, upon which was a steaming bowl of broth and several slices of chunky, freshly-baked bread. It smelled delicious.

'Here you go, son,' she said.

At the sight of it Steven's belly gave an embarrassing rumble. Putting his mug down on the floor, he picked up a spoon. The old woman winked at him.

He couldn't remember when he had last been this hungry – couldn't remember when he had been hungry, in fact. Suddenly there was a ravenous beast inside his stomach which was growling and pawing at the sight and smell of the food.

Without hesitating, he tucked in.

The broth was hot and flavoursome, the bread thick and hearty. For a while Steven forgot everything else, so absorbed was he in eating. He spooned the broth eagerly into his mouth, taking huge bites of the bread, pausing now and again only to slurp from the mug by his feet.

At last, when it was all gone, he gave a contented sigh. He felt good; wonderful, in fact. The food had filled him with a tingling glow that spread outwards from his stomach to his fingers and toes. He felt warm and deeply comforted.

'Is that better, now?' the woman asked.

Steven nodded and smiled. 'Thanks. That was wonderful - '

Then, abruptly, he yawned widely. 'Ooops! I'm sorry - '

'Never mind,' the woman told him. 'You rest, now.'

'I think - ' All of a sudden, he felt exhausted. He slid deeper into the chair, a luxurious tiredness unrolling over him; not the exhaustion that comes at the end of a long and restless journey, but the well-earned weariness of a day's work well done.

'Rest, now,' the woman's voice came again gently, and he felt a blanket being tucked in around him. 'Sleep.'

Steven fell into slumber. He dreamed.

He dreamed of things he had never seen, bright flashes of places and people that came and went like reflections in an unending hall of mirrors.

He saw a smoke-wracked den where prostrate figures lay immobile on mats of straw, eyes wide and unblinking, fixed in their addled visions. A grotesquely fat figure squatted before a low table, chortling with glee as the rings clicked on his fingers. He saw the Wells of Dreams, shining with light, and a figure who stood above it, face tilted downwards to see – and then it plunged its face into the dark bright water, and *began to* –

Steven turned away.

Dreams, so many dreams...

*Who would steal them? And why?*

Dreams were powerful. If you had many dreams, you gathered power...why would the Lord of Nightmares want that?

Dream himself stronger...

If enough people dreamed of something, it grew bigger, Orion had said. Over time, it could even become a thing in itself, greater than the dream...

So if you could make everyone dream of you...you'd be...

You'd be –

Ruler. *The* Ruler, alone and unchallenged.

Ruler of Dreams, and the Dreamland.

Or Ruler of -

Steven awoke with a start.

'I know!' he cried. 'I know what he's doing!'

The woman was sitting at the kitchen table, a cup of tea by her elbow. 'There, now. Feeling better?'

'Yes – it's – I am, thank you – I have to – I know what he's going to do!'

Somehow, he had to get a message to Orion. He had to go!

He made to get up, then a sudden sound made him stop.

Tick. Tick. Tick.

Slow, gentle, even.

Tick. Tick.

Steven glanced around.

Had it been there the whole time, or was he just noticing it now?

*Where's it coming from?*

He looked at the wall.

Over the stove was a white circle with twelve black numbers arranged in perfect intervals around the edge. Steven had seen hundreds like it before, in the other world, but this was the first one he'd seen in the Dreamland.

It was this that gave forth the soft, almost imperceptible ticking. And there were no hands.

Steven looked at the old woman. The woman who lived in a cottage in the middle of nowhere, who had invited him in, fed him, and watched over him while he slept.

He needed to ask.

'Are you-?'

'Fix my Clock for me, son,' she interrupted him gently. 'Once it's going again, we won't have any vermin going around stealing dreams. Can you do that for me?'

Steven swallowed, then nodded. 'Yes. I can do that for you.'

There was a knock on the door.

Steven jumped up, the blanket crumpling to the floor.

His head felt fuzzy, as though he'd been sleeping for a long time. The kitchen was dark and empty. Rain lashed the windows.

He rubbed his eyes, blinking, and went to the door.

Then he gasped for joy. 'Orion!'

The black-and-white cat stood on the doorstep, looking thoroughly wretched. His fur was plastered to his body, and his whiskers were drenched and bedraggled. Even his luminous eyes had lost their usual gleam.

'Steven,' he sighed. 'Am I glad to see you!'

'I was outside at the House,' Steven explained. 'I saw the Well, and then the Dream Thief appeared, and - '

'There's no time,' Orion exclaimed crossly. 'Come on, we have to go. You can tell me on the way.'

'But – okay, wait a minute, I have to - ' Steven glanced over his shoulder, looking for the old woman. He had to say goodbye.

There was no sign of her. Dust covered the furniture, and there were cobwebs on the kettle and stove.

It looked like no-one had lived there for a long time.

'I - ' Steven shook his head. 'Never mind.'

He pulled the door closed behind him.

They crossed the meadow. The pelting rain flung itself against their exposed forms, an army trying to drive them back. The limp grass was soaked, the earth damp and sliding beneath their feet. Clouds the colour of steel strangled the sun.

Steven started shivering as the icy rain got through his clothes. He crossed his arms over his chest, keeping his head down. In a few moments he was soaked through.

Orion led him to a small copse of trees at the edge of the meadow. An enormous white stallion stood there, reins looped around a branch, and by its side was a man dressed in a mottled green robe and with a fierce, hawk-like expression.

'Hey,' Steven said. 'I know you!'

'This,' Orion said, 'is Gaberlunzie.'

The man drew back his hood. He had bright blue eyes, a large hooked nose, and a rough scar that crested one cheek. His black hair was sodden with rain.

'The Sleepwalker,' he rumbled in deep tones. 'A pleasure to make your acquaintance.'

To Steven's embarrassment, he dropped to one knee.

'Er- it's nice to - ' Steven said. 'You don't have to - '

'It is an honour to meet you,' Gaberlunzie went on. 'It is rare indeed, in these times, to meet a Sleepwalker.'

'I've seen you before, haven't I?' Steven said.

'Gaberlunzie is a most talented tracker,' Orion told him. 'He has been following you to ensure your safety.'

'So that's what you were doing!' Steven remembered the shock of seeing him at the fairground, and then again in the shadows at the house. 'I thought you might be the Dream Thief.'

'At both times I could sense he was near,' Gaberlunzie admitted. 'It was my task to ensure you did not come to harm. On the second count, I must admit, I failed. I did not realise he would be strong enough to enter the garden.'

'None of us did,' Orion murmured. 'You were not to blame.'

'Orion, I'm sorry,' Steven said. 'I shouldn't have gone outside – I didn't think - '

'It doesn't matter,' the cat said. 'You survived, which is the important thing. And now we have discovered the Dream Thief's lair at last.'

Gaberlunzie went to his horse and unloosed the reins. It whinnied and shook its mane, sending droplets of water flying.

'Mount up!' he said, swinging one leg over and sliding deftly into the saddle. He held an arm out for Steven.

'Okay - ' Steven gripped his hand and found himself lifted effortlessly up and behind Gaberlunzie, perching somewhat awkwardly on the stallion's back.

'Er – is it going to be heavy with both of us?'

Gaberlunzie laughed fiercely and patted the horse's neck. 'He has borne heavier burdens than you, never fear. Come, let us be away!'

With a meow Orion sprang up and onto Steven's lap, and he suddenly found himself with an armful of soaking wet cat.

'Yuk – Orion, you're freezing - '

Orion eyed him balefully. 'I don't like it any more than you do, believe me.'

Then they were away.

The ground fell away with each thunderous beat of the horse's mighty hooves. Steven gripped tightly onto Gaberlunzie's robe, Orion hanging between his arms.

Rain lashed him in the face. The wind of their passage howled in his ears.

'Orion!' he shouted. 'I know why the Dream Thief wants the dreams! I know what he's trying to do!'

'I know!' Orion called back. 'They want to tip the Balance and make the Lord of Nightmares the ruler!'

'How – how did you know?' Steven said. He was almost disappointed that Orion had figured it out. He wanted to be the one to do it. 'I thought I - '

'There's a lot of things I know,' Orion said, somehow looking smug despite the fact he was soaked through and clinging onto Steven for dear life.

'Actually,' he said after a moment, relenting, 'it was my Mistress who finally pieced it together. If you have enough dreams in your possession, you can – transform them somehow, bend them to your will. And that's what he will do, if we give him the chance.'

'If,' Steven murmured. He held on tighter to Gaberlunzie's robe.

The ground fell away beneath them. They passed through meadows and fields, leapt over streams, ducked under low-hanging branches. They seemed to ride forever.

*How much further??*

At the end of the road, the Dream Thief.

Steven kept changing his mind; one part of him was eager, desperate almost, to come to the end, to finally face the Dream Thief and stop him; another shrank away, trying to put off the final moments as long as he could. He swung between the two like a pendulum.

Gradually, the ground began to change. The grass dropped away and they were riding across bare moorland. Stark and bare it was; the pounding rain made the gorse and brackish heather treacherous underfoot; and stunted shrubs, thick rocks, were the only things for the eye to catch on. Here and there a few blasted trees cast scarecrow limbs against the sky.

Drop by drop, the light seemed to trickle away around them, so that they rode through a pale, sickly gloom. Steven began to shiver. A chill grew inside of him, as though something was drawing out his warmth, sapping his strength.

Then they came to a halt.

The horse shied, whinnying in distress. Gaberlunzie shushed it tenderly, stroking its mane. Steven looked over his shoulder.

They were at the base of a hill. It was bare, wet earth with a few straggling strands of grass on the slope.

At the top was a faint, humped shape. Steven squinted, trying to make it out. It seemed to change shape as he looked at it. First it was a long hall with the roof gouged open and the bare timbers showing; then it was the broken remnants of a stone tower; then a thick black haze that shifted like the clicking mandibles of a venomous insect.

'We're here,' Orion said.

One by one, they dismounted. Gaberlunzie tied his horse to a nearby stump.

'What is this place?' Steven asked.

'It was a grand feasting-hall, once,' Gaberlunzie said, one hand on the hilt of his sword. His voice was full of sorrow and regret. 'A place of merriment and feasting.

'Then the Lord of Nightmares took it for his own, and gave it to his servant. Only crows have feasted there since.'

'That's – er - cheery,' Steven muttered, shading his eyes. The hall – if that was what it was – continued to shimmer and shift like smoke.

For a moment they paused, the three of them, looking upwards, very small under the overhanging sky and the looming shadow of the Dream Thief's hideaway. Then, as one, they began to ascend the hill.

Immediately Steven started to have trouble breathing. The air grew thick, as though he waded through sludge.

By his side, he could hear Gaberlunzie gasping. Orion was panting somewhere near his ankles.

The rough, slumped building swam closer, then retreated again. The broken timbers thrust at them like a jagged fist.

Gaberlunzie grunted in pain.

'Are you all right?' Steven asked.

The tracker's face was drawn and lined, and he held a hand to his side as if wounded.

'I am – well. It is the –interference.'

'It will - get worse,' Orion said slowly. 'He will attempt - to stop us entering.'

Steven gritted his teeth. Each step was now a monumental effort. He willed his feet to keep moving. He felt as if someone was running molten lead into his bones.

'We – can't – stop,' he said. 'Must – go on.'

Orion muttered. Gaberlunzie was in too much pain to speak.

A moment later he gasped and slumped forward.

Steven knelt by his side.

'It's – nothing.' He gripped Steven's arm. 'I – cannot go on. I am - sorry.'

'It's okay,' Steven reassured him. 'Stay - here.'

Eyes closed tightly, Gaberlunzie gave a nod of assent, then collapsed, breath rasping in his lungs.

Steven and Orion went on.

The ruined hall grew closer by inches. Cartwheels of darkness spun across his vision.

'Are you – how – are you -?' Orion coughed wetly, as though he were choking on a hairball.

'I'm – fine,' Steven managed to laugh. 'Nothing – to it.'

Was he really going forwards? The hill was tilting, the horizon sliding away.

'I- '

It sprang up before them, leaping suddenly forward like a snake lunging from a thicket.

It was huge, Steven saw – no, small, smaller than a telephone box – the walls were wriggling, sliding, its weight bore on him, crushed him down ruthlessly.

*Must – touch - door-*

Foot by foot, he dragged himself forward. His mouth was as dry as dust. He had been walking in the desert for years, searching for water...

Everything spun. The darkness was knotting in front of him.

Which was the ground? Which was the sky?

*Think!!*

He clamped his eyes shut, pressing out with his hands. They had to be close now. Very close.

'Steven...' Orion weaved back and forth. 'Can't – see - '

He collapsed.

Steven –

- touched the door.

The black haze vanished. It was just an abandoned hall, walls crumbling, door hanging open.

Inside the rough stone floor was covered in ash and dirt. Broken tables were scattered against the  walls. Chairs leaned spasmodically to and fro. Along the walls, metal sconces held burnt-out torches .

At the end of the hall, gleaming in the shadows like a full moon, was the clock.

The Clock of Hours.

It was the same as Steven's grandfather clock at home.

Exactly the same.

Seeing it here, in the Dream Thief's lair, gathered a rush of homesickness in him. He felt the sky above, the walls open on either side, and knew that here, now, was the end of his journey. For better or for worse. It was, indeed, time to finish it.

The hands of the Clock were fixed at midnight.

*Fix my Clock for me, son.*

Quickly, he unhooked the oak panels, swinging them outwards. There was no key.

Gone.

Missing?

*Where-?*

A cold, high laugh rang out.

'Looking for this?'

A man in a shimmering robe stepped out of the shadows. In one hand he held the black sack. In the other he held the key, small and silver and shining.

The Dream Thief.

'Give that back!' Steven exclaimed.

The Dream Thief shook his head. 'No, I don't think so. It's mine now. And so are *these*.'

He shook the sack roughly and Steven heard a chorus of despairing cries, as though it were a bag of kittens he was intent on drowning.

'You're hurting them,' he said quietly.

'They are mine, to do with as I please,' the Dream Thief hissed. 'They belong to me. Me and my Master. And you, little Sleepwalker, have come to the end of your quest.'

He tucked the key away and drew back the hood of his robe.

Steven gasped. 'You!'

Lokin laughed contemptuously. 'Me!'

He bore the face of the man Steven had met at the fairground, with long chestnut hair and a mischievous grin, but as Steven watched he passed his hand down from brow to chin in one long motion.

His face changed. It became cruel and hard, the bones standing out under the chalk-white skin, and his eyes burned in their sockets, red-rimmed and mad.

'But - ' Steven started. 'You – look completely different.'

He had been fooled. There was no way he could have known who the Dream Thief really was. Lokin had been right under his nose, laughing at him all the time.

'Different?' Lokin laughed again. 'Yes, indeed. Told you I was a trickster, didn't I? Well, now there is no need for pretence. Here I am.

'And here you are.'

Slowly, deliberately, he began to creep closer to Steven, licking his lips hungrily.

Steven backed away, lifting his hands up. He couldn't hope to win in a battle against Lokin; he was too powerful to fight here. He only had one chance...

'A boy like you, thinking he could beat me!' Lokin jabbered furiously. 'Me! I, who had the vision, the power! I who chose to serve the greatest of them all, the Lord of Nightmares! And when I deliver my cargo to him, he will tip the Balance and destroy the others forever. Then we will rule this world, and yours too, boy. You just wait and see.'

Closer he came, face twitching feverishly, fingers flexing and tightening on the black sack. Steven was running out of time.

*I have to try.*

'You're right,' he said eagerly, 'I can't beat you. You're too strong for me. How about giving me a chance, though, Lokin? What do you say?'

The Dream Thief stared at him, eyes bulging.

'Come on,' Steven said coaxingly. 'You said I was a fighter, remember? Well how about a fighting chance? What have you got to lose?'

Lokin frowned, tongue darting out like a lizard. He shifted from one foot to the other.

'Come on,' Steven said witheringly. 'You're not *scared*, are you?'

Lokin snarled in anger and for one moment Steven thought he had gone too far.

The Dream Thief drew himself up and gave a strange bark of laughter. 'A chance? A fighting chance? Very well, why not. Let it not be said that I am not a sporting man.'

He ripped open the black sack and plunged his hand inside. Through the opening Steven caught a glimpse of the glowing spheres of dreams, struggling against their captivity, falling over one another in their haste to be free.

Lokin shoved them back in, muttering furiously to himself. 'No – no – not this one - no – ah! *Yes!*'

He pulled out a dream clutched tightly in his fingers. Shining with rosy pink light, threaded with rich purple, it strained against his grasp.

Lokin barked with laughter again. 'You'll like this one, boy. I know who this was intended for...she had a doll's house when she was young, yes? It's a memory of that, but I think we'll make a few changes!'

He opened his hand and the light swelled and grew. The pink and purple shades became a murky, sludge-like hue, the colour of plants gone rotten and decaying at the bottom of an ancient well.

Lokin plunged a finger in and stirred it as though it were a cauldron, sending eddies of filth into the air around him.

Then he grinned malevolently. 'Ready? One, two, three...'

An invisible hook slammed into Steven's chest and he was wrenched head-first into the dream.

He gagged; it was like being thrown into a freezing marsh. Thick, cloying, it gripped him with no chance of escape. He thrashed this way and that, but it did no good. Somewhere close, Lokin was laughing.

Then he was standing at the end of a bed.

A girl was sitting upright before him, sobbing miserably. Her flaming red hair fell forward over his clasped knees, hiding her face.

*Is that –*

She looked familiar. Had he met her before?

'Are you okay?' Steven asked. 'What's happened?'

In shock, the girl looked up. A smattering of freckles covered her cheeks. Her expression changed from surprise, then confusion, and then passed into a strange mix of fear and wonder.

It was the girl from the tower.

'You,' she whispered. 'Why do I keep dreaming of you?'

'It's alright,' Steven told her. 'I'm going to help you.'

The girl bent forward again, weeping. 'He took it! He took my dream!'

There was an icy giggle, like nails being dragged across a window, and the girl disappeared.

'Looks like you're going to the Funhouse after all, Steven!'

Then he found himself in an enormous room.

The walls towered over his head. Long windows let in a little light. Driving rain pounded against the glass. There came the low, mournful howl of the wind.

Around him the floor was covered with toys.

Children's toys.

Yet they were impossibly large. There was a hideous doll, head forward on its chest as though sleeping, with bloated pink limbs and a head that was almost bald except for a few lank strands of hair still clinging grimly on.

Nearby was a vast wooden rocking-horse, daubed in gaudy colour as if it had gone mad and escaped from a carousel. It wore a wild, demented grin, and several of its teeth had been gouged out.

By its side was a fire-engine with broken windows and a punctured tire. To Steven, it was almost life-size.

Lokin's voice echoed from somewhere in the darkness. 'Oh Steven, you don't look like you're having any fun! Let's fix that, shall we?'

There was a wet, rubbery, wrenching sound and the giant doll swivelled its head towards Steven. One black eye looked off to the left; the other was rolled back into its socket.

'Uuuuuhhh,' it moaned.

'Oh no,' Steven whispered.

Slowly, the doll got to its feet. Once upright it was even larger and with awkward, thumping steps it lunged towards him.

He dived to one side as it raised one massive limb.

'Eeeeeehhhhh!' it roared.

Its arm smashed down where he had been standing only a moment before. The doll lifted its arm and, finding nothing at the end, roared again. 'Aaaaaeeeeeehhh!'

*I'm keeping away from that!*

He ran behind it, dodging around the fire-engine.

With a blare of harsh sound the siren snapped on. Steven flinched in shock as the orange and blue lights flared and the engine roared. Its wheels spun and it shot over the ground, listing on the broken tire.

*Need to find somewhere to hide!!*

He made for the rocking-horse, thinking to crawl underneath it and take refuge, but there came an awful crunch of wood and the head tilted downwards, fixing Steven with an empty stare. The painted lips curved wider, leering with menace.

'I hope you like what I've done with the place!' Lokin cackled.

Steven scrambled back, away from the rocking-horse. The doll was lumbering towards him again, arms raised to crush him. The fire-engine shot around behind him, siren wailing.

'*Having fun yet?*' Lokin shrieked, and burst into laughter.

Steven had nowhere to go. He was trapped.

He needed something. Anything.

*What can I use??*

Before he could think the doll was upon him once more, arms sweeping down like falling tree-trunks.

In desperation, he dived forward, flinging himself between the legs of the doll. He felt the enormous thump as the huge arms hit the ground behind him.

'Uuuuuhhhh?'

'Not bad, Steven!' Lokin cried. 'You're quite good at this! Tell you what, pick a card!'

There was a sharp, high whistle and a playing card shot out of the shadows and sliced across his arm.

'Ow!' Steven clutched the wound, feeling the blood welling up between his fingers.

*I'm cut!!*

Lokin giggled.

The fire-engine raced by, almost running over his foot. Steven was forced to dart back, pressing himself against the wall.

'How about this?' Lokin called. More cards slammed into the wall by his head – one, two, three - and Steven dived to one side away, panting.

His thoughts raced. How could he stop Lokin?

'Or this one?'

A playing card *snicked* into the floor by his foot. It exploded in a cloud of foul-smelling smoke that engulfed his face, making him cough and splutter. Coughing and spluttering in the acrid fumes, he staggered away.

*I need –*

The fire-truck thundered past, leaning to one side.

The rocking-horse had begun to sway back and forth, still grinning.

*I need – I need -*

The doll was advancing, each ponderous step making the ground shake.

*I – I –*

Cards whistled over his head like knives.

*- can't.*

Sick at heart, Steven held his hands up in surrender. 'Alright! I give up! You win!'

Everything in the room halted, then slowly came to a stop. The dream dissolved around him.

He was back in the ravaged hall.

Lokin crowed in triumph. 'You see! You cannot beat me!'

Steven rubbed his arm where Lokin had cut him. He felt cold and wretched. To think that this was it; that it would end like this. That he just didn't have the skill.

'Now, Steven,' Lokin said in a mock-sorrowful tone, 'this *is* the end, I'm sorry to say.'

From within the folds of his robe he drew a small, odd-shaped doll. It was stitched together from rough pieces of cloth. The face was blank.

'What's – what's that?' Steven said.

*Keep him talking –*

*- for what? I've lost!*

Lokin waved the doll back and forth. 'Can't you see? Oh, very well.'

He flicked his hand and the burnt-out torches on the wall roared to life, crackling and hissing. One flamed behind Steven's head.

'Didn't anyone ever tell you not to give anything away here?' Lokin said.

He slipped something onto his hand and held it up.

It was the trick buzzer that he'd used on Steven at the fairground.

And it had Steven's blood on it.

Dimly, he heard Merryweather's warning...*Terrible bad luck for anything to get a piece of you here, if they wish you ill...*

*Terrible bad luck...*

*He's planned this all along,* Steven thought. *Right from when we met.*

Lokin smiled at him, a strange, almost gentle smile, and pushed the pin into the doll's chest.

Steven cried out in pain. A hot flare of pain burst inside him.

'Oh, does it hurt?' Lokin said. He jabbed the pin into the doll's leg.

'*Argh!!*' His leg sagged beneath him. It felt like someone had struck a match on his thigh.

That was it. No more...

He had nothing left.

*I'm sorry, Orion...I'm sorry, everyone...*

Lokin's eyes burned like hot stones. He jabbed the pin into the doll's back.

A sharp slash of fire.

Strength was leaving him, stealing away even as the cold crept insidiously in. He wanted to lie down, to rest and never rise again.

'You're going to pieces, Steven,' Lokin hissed.

Pieces...

*He really has a horrible voice,* a small part of him said.

*Now you have a piece of me wherever you go...*

*What was that?*

The pain was growing, mushrooming inside him...he couldn't stay up much longer...

*Pick a card, Steven...*

*Pick a card....*

*- a card!!*

And then Steven knew.

He thrust his hand into his back pocket. Closed it around what waited there.

What he'd carried all this way. What Lokin himself had given him.

Pulled it out.

Leaning on the wall for support, hopping slightly on one leg, Steven held out his fist.

Lokin watched him amusedly. 'Oh yes? What's this? One final surprise?'

'You could say that,' Steven muttered.

'Well, let's see it,' Lokin said. 'Let's see, Sleepwalker.'

Slowly, Steven opened his hand. 'Didn't anyone ever tell you not to give anything away?'

It was Lokin's card.

Flat, white, it lay becalmed in the centre of Steven's palm. The picture of Lokin grinned underneath the torchlight. It winked at Steven.

For an instant, Lokin stared at it in shock. Then his eyes widened as he understood.

'Is this your card, Lokin?' Steven asked.

Dropping the doll, Lokin darted forward. '*No!!*'

And Steven thrust the card into the blazing torch behind him.

Lokin screamed.

The sleeves of his robe erupted in flame. Lokin whirled and spun, flapping his arms desperately, t trying to extinguish them. It did no good.

In a matter of moments he became a living torch.

Shrieking, he ran back and forth, calling for help. Beseeching the Lord of Nightmares for aid.

Nothing happened. The Lord had cast his servant aside.

Steven closed his eyes and turned away until it was over.

When he opened them again, all that remained was a pile of sickly green ash on the floor.

Steven limped over to one of the broken chairs. Taking hold of a loose leg, he wrenched it free. He used it to poke through Lokin's remains.

At the bottom of the pile of ash he found the key. He dragged it free and blew on it until it gleamed again.

'You lose, Lokin,' he murmured.

There came a long breath of wind through the hall. It touched Lokin's ashes, sending them swirling up through the open roof. In a few moments, there was nothing left to show he'd been there at all.

Steven went to the black sack. Gripping the drawstring, he pulled it open wide.

Out poured the light. It blazed, dazzled, plunged outwards like a waterfall.

It fell over him in a hundred different shades, a crescendo of dreams, and each dream had a voice.

*Thank you*, they said. *Thank you...*

It took a long time.

When the sack was empty, he crumpled it up and kicked it away into a corner. Then he thought better of it, and took down one of the torches. The sack burned slowly, and with a rancid stench that made his eyes water.

The Clock of Hours waited, mute and still.

Steven looked at the wonderful mechanism inside.

This clock had counted all the moments of his life, right from when he was born. It had always been there, he realised, watching over him.

As it watched over everyone, he supposed.

And how much longer would it tick, he wondered? How many more moments would he have? How many more sunrises and sunsets?

Who could say?

He didn't have the answers.

He knew who did, though.

He looked at the key in his hand. It nestled there, so small. So small a thing.

His, now, if he wanted it. The Clock could be his, too.

All sorts of things could be his, if he wished.

The silver clock-face gleamed.

Steven shook his head, and laughed a little, and put in the key.

He turned it seven times to the right.

And the Clock of Hours struck midnight.

It struck the hour with a ringing of silver chimes.

At the first stroke the ruined hall disappeared. Steven saw Gaberlunzie raise himself from the hillside, stretch his limbs. He raised his fingers in salute.

The second chime came.

Now he was somewhere high, looking out over the Dreamland. There were points of light glowing like fireflies in the dusk as the dreams, freed at last from their cruel prison, spread out across the land. The dreamers were free once more. The Balance had been maintained.

The third chime sounded. Then the fourth.

Merryweather hopped and capered. 'See my boy, see! I knew you'd do it! Yes indeed!'

The fifth.

The three figures were seated on their thrones. The Maiden of Sleep and the Earl of Dreams were smiling, satisfied. The Lord of Nightmares had his face turned to the wall.

'Thank you,' they said. 'Thank you, Steven.'

The sixth chime.

The old woman in her kitchen, bread cooking in the oven, kettle whistling chirpily. The clock on the wall had its hands restored.

The seventh.

The red-haired girl slept peacefully in her bed. Everything back in its rightful place.

Would he see her again?

*Could he?*

The eighth chime sounded.

After all, he was a Sleepwalker, wasn't he? He walked in dreams.

The ninth chime.

And if he didn't find her one night, there was always tomorrow. And the night after, and the night  after that...

The tenth.

He was rising now, through the layers of sleep. The waking world drew near.

The eleventh chime sounded.

'Not bad, Steven,' Orion said. His fur was smooth again and his eyes glowed like electric lanterns.  'Not bad at all. See you next time!'

He winked.

Steven thought, *next time? Yeah, right -*

Then the twelfth chime sounded.

And he woke up.

Printed in Great Britain
by Amazon